BADLANDS CURSED

WADE PETERSON

PROLOGUE

The ornithopter dropped in a stomach-clenching free-fall before its engine caught and slammed the majordomo against the seat. The majordomo's craft shot away from the city-ship *Caliphate of the Clouds*. He guided the craft with a steady hand, circling until the burning airship finally kissed the desert sands, breaking up with the scream of metal and the roar of exploding fuel.

The Caliph's corpse roasted below him. The majordomo smiled.

A delicious fate, the fat lecherous bastard killed by a *hareem* girl in his bedroom—the Creator's own sister, if one believed the Caliph's demented samurai. Kikuchiyo, the Blood Weeper, had been outside the bedroom door and yet not intervened. Interesting. Did this mean the Creator's control over his avatars had slipped also? This was opportunity.

The majordomo, ex-majordomo he reminded himself, banked away from the wreck and set a course for a nearby supply depot. The city-ship was gone but the Caliphate itself was already his; bribes, promises, betrayals, and assassinations had put him in near total authority, and with the Caliph dead, the last barrier had been removed. But to keep power he would need to control this new god, the Creator's sister. She would travel for Paradise City, and the Caliphate already had agents in its Undercity, its naval squadrons, the populace, even the ruling council. Yes, it was time. For he too was an avatar of the Creator and this was his moment. The sister was the key, this Jasmine.

He reached for the radio and set his plan in motion.

PART I

1

____

Everything was fine until their deader broke.

Their stolen 'thopter shook and lurched sideways. Jasmine braced herself in the cockpit's seat and against her better judgment, looked over the side. The desert scrub raced underneath them, too fast to make out individual bushes, and getting closer.

Jasmine shouted over the whining twin turbines, but Helgo didn't hear her. She reached out and tapped Helgo's shoulder and pointed to the ground. He screamed something she couldn't understand as he fought the 'thopter's control yoke with his right hand and rubbed the instrument panel with his left like a cowboy settling a spooked horse. Her stomach flipped as Helgo over-corrected first one way, then another. Finally, he brought them back under control, though the ground still grew closer with every passing second. He pushed the throttle forward and the 'thopter surged higher.

Helgo let out a breath and shouted over his shoulder. "The power's fading. I'm coaxing what's left in our deader and trying to keep the flow even, but I don't know how long it'll last."

Jasmine looked over the side at the ground pulling away and let out a breath. Then the right engine's pitch changed and dissonance twisted her eardrums. The 'thopter shuddered and the engine began spewing smoke. Helgo adjusted the throttle, then the left engine burst into flames.

"Fuck!" Helgo shouted, and Jasmine cinched up her seat's harness. Helgo pulled the throttle back and the engines went silent, though still smoking.

"Can we make it down?"

"I'll try feathering it, but this ground's shit for landing," Helgo muttered, then punched the fuselage. "Fucking Caliphate deaders!"

Jasmine put a hand on his shoulder. "Focus, Helgo. You can do it." He nodded and leaned forward, concentrating.

Jasmine craned her neck and looked from side to side. The ground filled her vision with endless jagged rocks, low hills, treacherous bushes, and shards of tree trunks ready to smash, snag, or spear them. Then a path appeared, no more than a dry stream bed. Jasmine pointed over Helgo's shoulder, and he nodded, wresting the control yoke.

"Almost there. Hang on," Helgo said and made quick jerking movements on the yoke as the 'thopter slewed from side to side. The stream bed disappeared, and a giant invisible hand threw her forward. In slow motion, the 'thopter spun on its belly, throwing up a wave of fine white sand. The scent of burnt flesh filled her nostrils. The light went dim and metal screeched. She closed her eyes and waited for a sudden pain to pierce her. Then everything stopped.

She cautiously opened her eyes as the light grew brighter. Her heart pounded, and she suddenly couldn't breathe fast enough. She mashed at the seat release and threw back the canopy. The 'thopter was partially buried in the sand, but the engines had stopped smoking. She gathered herself to jump from her seat, then stopped as she remembered Helgo. The necrosonic engineer hung in his seat's restrains, head slumped.

"Helgo!" Jasmine shouted. His head lolled, and he let out a moan.

Jasmine reached down and fought with the release, catching his weight before his head could smash into the instrument panel.

"Come on, let's go," she said. Jasmine got her arms under his and pulled him out, the little man surprisingly heavy. She dragged him from the cockpit, collapsing beside him and shivering as the adrenaline wore off. From the 'thopter, the deader mumbled and knocked against its restraints.

"Sis-taaah ... Sis-taaah."

Helgo coughed and rolled to his side. "Never heard them talk before."

Jasmine shrugged. "Fucking Caliphate deaders," she said and turned back to the 'thopter.

"It seems to know you."

Jasmine sighed and looked back at Helgo's dust-smeared face. "Yeah, I get that a lot."

She rummaged through the 'thopter, searching for food, water, and weapons. Helgo braced himself against the fuselage and levered a panel open. Jasmine glanced over at him and the blackened, dessicated deader's body writhing within the 'thopter's engine compartment. Helgo twisted and jerked at cables running into the deader's torso and skull.

"You shouldn't do that," Jasmine said.

"What? It can't feel anything."

"You know that for sure? You hadn't heard one talk before either."

Helgo shrugged and tapped a tattoo on the deader's forehead, then put his ear close to the deader's chest. Jasmine shook her head and went back to scavenging items from the cockpit. She grabbed a cloth bundle speckled with blood and carried it into the sunlight before opening it. The bundle was made from a yellow party dress and held two guitar strings plus a plastic bag containing an off-white oily lump. Jasmine pocketed the strings, smoothed out the wrinkles in the dress, and left the baggie on a rock.

Somehow Cally had managed to keep her yellow party dress after the Caliph's men captured and brought them both to the *hareem*. Cally, who fought off deader hordes in the Badlands for months and taught Jasmine how to survive, accepted her new role as concubine as easily as putting on a new pair of slippers. Yet she saved the dress, her last tie to Jasmine's brother Ryan, and the guitar strings, their only memento from Bishop, who died getting them out of the Badlands. The oily ball in the plastic bag, well... Cally took to a concubine's life a bit too readily and got herself addicted to the hookah. She had been the ultimate survivor right up until she found herself looking at the Blood Weeper's sword poking out from her chest.

"Fuck a duck!" Helgo shouted. "There's nothing left in him!"

Jasmine looked back at Helgo putting a hand to his back as he straightened. "Induced noise from somewhere burnt him out, either bad cable routing or a strong nearby power source? I don't know. It's *no bueno.* This deader's out of juice."

"Meaning what?"

He wiped his brow. "It'll be a corpse soon."

"I thought deaders couldn't die."

"Who told you that nonsense?" He waved his hand. "Deaders are just batteries with an appetite for flesh. Whoever installed this sad bastard in a 'thopter engine ought to be shot." Helgo shook his head. "Should have been matched pairs, or an over-sized single body at least."

"Well if he's a battery, can't we recharge him?" Jasmine asked.

"With what? They only eat humans, and I ain't volunteering."

Jasmine walked over to the 'thopter and peered into the engine compartment. The deader looked at her with filmy eyes. Black cracked lips and a swollen gray tongue hissed at her. Beneath the restraints and wires, the deader's skin stretched thin over limbs little more than sticks with knobs for joints. Even the deaders in the Badlands looked better than this poor thing.

"Maybe I can help," she said.

"I wouldn't–" Helgo said but before he could say anything further, Jasmine had drawn a small scalpel from her belt. She winced against the quick bite and held her bleeding thumb over the deader's mouth. Her blood spattered on its blackened teeth and the tongue swept it away. Then the deader jerked with a sudden breath and surged against its restraints. Electricity flared a split second before a sound like a shotgun blast sent her ears ringing.

Helgo's arms hooked under her shoulders and pulled her from the compartment, sending them tumbling to the ground. Jasmine put an elbow into Helgo's stomach and he let go with a grunt. Smoke began pouring from the hatch.

"Are you daft? *Loco?* What did you do to it?" Helgo said.

"I tried bringing it back to life," she said.

"You can't—" Then the deader screamed. Through the smoke, the deader's blackened head and torso turned pink though the limbs remained leathery and dark. Brown eyes bored through her as the deader screamed again, then abruptly fell silent. The flesh withered and turned black before her eyes until it was just a deader again, or rather a mummi-fied corpse, since its chest no longer rose or fell.

Good one, Jas.

"Dammit," Jasmine said.

Helgo's stare alternated between her bleeding thumb and the corpse. Jasmine stood, waiting for him to tear into her for fucking up or else run away screaming.

"Well, it wasn't like it was going to be useful anyway. Lucky thing it didn't catch on fire," he finally said.

"It worked on trees and bushes in the Badlands," Jasmine said. "It worked on you."

Helgo rubbed his chest where Jasmine had healed him on the Caliph's airship. He noticed her gaze and quickly went about waving away the residual smoke from the engine compartment before peering inside. "Deaders are too far gone to be changed back to anything human."

"But I've..." The words died on her tongue as the memory came unbidden. Her blood-smeared thighs. The Caliph's naked body. The drugs clearing from her mind as the cruel man standing over her morphed into a confused and shocked Ryan.

"What?" Helgo asked.

"Nothing. Forget it," she said.

Helgo didn't look like he believed her, but he only sighed and poked at the deader with a finger.

Jasmine pushed past him to gather up the things Cally had left behind. Cally dead. Bishop dead. Both killed trying to help her and nothing left to remember them by but two guitar strings and a party dress. Of all the useless things to have in the middle of a desert! Jasmine coiled the strings around her wrist and tied the loose ends together with a length of yellow ribbon from Cally's dress. It wasn't much as memorials went, but it was portable. She gave her wrist a shake and the bracelet settled comfortably against her skin. The sun hung low in the sky, turning the sand around them burnt orange while the sky darkened to cobalt.

She wiped at the sweat streaming down her head, surprised for a moment as fingertips touched stubble, a reminder of her attempted rebellion in the Caliph's harem. She quickly re-wrapped her headscarf.

"Let's go, Helgo."

The necrosonic engineer squatted before a pile of wires and junked metal. He poked at some pieces before wiping his hands on his t-shirt and giving the pile a kick, sending a metal scrap tumbling across the sand.

"Might as well. Hopefully it ain't much farther. Any more than a week and we're shit outta luck."

Jasmine rubbed at her bracelet. "One problem at a time, Helgo."

IN THE BADLANDS, they had followed the red lights of radio towers to Paradise City. There were no towers in this part of the desert so they followed lights of a different sort. High overhead, cabin lights from silent airships stood out against the featureless night sky, a sky with no moon or stars yet somehow glowing like a TV tuned to a black screen.

"You're sure those ships aren't with the Caliphate?" she asked.

"Nah, they don't run ships that big or run convoys like Paradise City does," he pointed at three moving lights. "That's probably two heavy cargo lifters and a gunship escort, coming out of the Badlands or trading with some other outpost."

"Like the settlers, the cannibals?"

"More like enclaves, people desperate enough to go scavenging in the wastes for deaders, raw materials, and artifacts in exchange for food and manufactured goods. Smart enough not to take on gunships armed with cannon and shields."

At the end of the next day's march over the sands, the horizon took on a glow which spurred them on. The glow resolved into sharp, bright lights as they grew closer. At a distance, the city could easily be mistaken for a small mountain with rounded sides and flattened top, except this mountain floated some hundred feet above the ground. Buildings large and small ringed the city's top half, all bathed in electric light that also highlighted the underbellies of orbiting airships.

"We made it," Jasmine said.

Helgo didn't respond. Jasmine turned, catching a glimpse of a frown before he gave a weary smile. "Let's sleep here for the night. We'll see if we can get up there in the morning."

"But it's moving away," Jasmine said.

"Catching up isn't the hard part, the city only travels at night. It won't go far in the next few hours."

"So what's the hard part?"

"You'll see tomorrow."

In the morning, the city hovered just over the next rise. Airships with brightly painted gondolas slung under gas bladders shrouded by outer envelopes of bright white canvass sailed into jutting framework docks. Beyond the docks, dun-colored brick buildings and modest skyscrapers of orange steel surrounded a colonnaded building with a blue rotunda at the city center. The docks and buildings dominated the highest ground, giving way to green terraces with orderly fields and orchards carved into the rock. Jasmine could make out individual waterfalls pouring onto the sands below.

A dark stain followed the city.

"Is that caused by the water?" Jasmine asked, pointing.

"No, that's a flood of a different type."

As Jasmine looked closer, she realized the dark stain was actually a mass of vehicles, tents, and people, crowded together, following in the city's shadow.

"They call it the Undercity," Helgo said.

2

Jasmine found herself pressed against unwashed bodies, carts, livestock, and shacks on wheels. Some of the more enterprising and desperate rushed ahead, eager to snap up prime real estate for themselves, for their masters, or for sale to laggards with means. The woman next to Jasmine wore rough-spun sand robes from head to foot, only her knobby hands were exposed as she pushed her belongings in a wheelbarrow. Jasmine tried smiling at her but the woman merely squinted and shied away. How did it ever come to pass that someone could be afraid of her, Jasmine wondered. Helgo elbowed her.

"Don't stare."

"I wasn't!"

"Most of 'em here are looking to get up there," Helgo said, pointing. "Or else make a living off the city and its followers. Rough life, and staring makes you a rube or a thug."

"So what are we?"

"Just minding our own business." Helgo curled a lip at a whip-thin teen drifting toward them. The boy changed course and disappeared into the crowd. "Mind your pockets too," Helgo said.

A fat ornithopter detached itself from a dock built into the city's underside and descended. Men and women with rifles and pikes ringed the craft's railing and alighted as it touched the sand, driving some overly-eager supplicants back and establishing a protective ring between the crowd and the 'thopter. Another man in a uniform set out a chair and a tattered umbrella between the two largest guards and sat down. The surrounding refugees shuffled their way to him, forming a line without being told. Helgo found a shaded spot near a tent and pointed at the ornithopter.

"That's our ride up," Helgo said. "Just have to get past the gate wardens."

Jasmine watched the growing line of refugees. The seated man turned the first hopeful away with a wave of his hand.

"Is that going to be a problem?" Jasmine asked.

"Not if you're useful. For a necro like me, not a problem. Not sure what they'll say about you."

Jasmine stared at the floating city's stone and metal underside hundreds of feet above. Bishop would have gotten them through with a secret handshake. Cally would have somehow charmed her way past the guards or traded in on her status as Ryan's girlfriend. Maybe the guards would let her up if they knew she was Ryan's sister?

A necro dressed in black robes embroidered with odd symbols whistled a Duran Duran song while leading a string of five deaders to the front. The last deader turned her way and faltered, jerking the others to a stop. It locked its filmy eyes on her and opened its mouth.

"Jasmine," Helgo said with a pained look. "Please don't fidget with that juju."

Jasmine pulled her hand away from the guitar string bracelet she had been absently sliding across her wrist. The necro cursed and jerked at the deader's lead. He sang softly, and the deaders all turned as if listening. The last one seemed to hesitate before turning with its fellows, and they shambled off. She met Helgo's eye. "With you everything is juju."

"Well, yeah, that's how it is. We don't want attention."

"So what's our plan?"

Helgo stared at the line for a few moments and let out a breath. "You're not going to like it."

～

HELGO DRAGGED her along the fringes as the last stragglers set up tents and tables in the city's shadow. Arguments broke out between hawkers while peddlers threw elbows and wedged their tables and carts along the trail as refugees flowed past. For their part, the refugees stopped to trade items for food, water, or better bribes. People glared up at the city as they talked, sometimes spitting as they did so. Traders smiled with the few wandering guards as they haggled, the smiles vanishing as soon as backs were turned. Hands rested on knife hilts or the odd pistol, the more affluent of the merchants used guards with pikes or rifles. Heads turned among the more desperate, taking her measure, noting the scalpels and knives strapped to her body, then the club at her waist before moving along. Jasmine stared and wondered how long this could go on before it all fell apart. Or had it fallen apart several times already?

A distant murmur came from the city above, and the Undercity paused for a moment before many shouted "castaway" and pointed. Overhead, a crowd had gathered at Paradise City's very edge. Many around her rushed to stand underneath the spectacle while others averted their gaze. One hawker started shouting names and taking bets. She turned to Helgo, who shook his head and nodded up at the drama. Watch. She turned just as a collective shout from the city reached them. A white bundle tumbled from the side. A thin scream reached her, louder as the bundle fell, ceasing as it hit the ground and bounced once.

The hawker made a comment and several around him laughed.

Helgo tapped her shoulder. "The jails in Paradise City are small and never crowded. Let's go, I think I recognize someone who can help." They walked to a tent off the main route, the area around it somehow free from jostling water-mongers and food stands. A weary-faced woman sat at the tent's entrance in plain but clean desert robes. She glanced up as they approached and straightened on her stool, a queen on her throne.

"Let me do the talking," he said. "Just stay alert and whatever you do, don't let her know you're Ryan's sister."

"Believe me, I'm trying to forget," Jasmine said.

"Kara Moore," Helgo said with a slight bow. "They call me Helgo. This is Jasmine, my traveling companion."

"A necro and a..." Kara's eyes narrowed and glanced around. "Well, you are who you are, aren't you? What can I do for you?"

"Perhaps we could discuss that inside," Helgo said.

Kara clucked her tongue and stood. "We could at that. Tatiana!"

A teenaged girl emerged and sat on the stool after a hand signal passed between her and Kara. Then the woman held the tent flap open and gestured for Helgo and Jasmine to enter. Inside, a hammock stand, canvass camp chairs, a small footlocker serving as a table, and a camping stove filled the space. Kara indicated they should sit, though she remained standing, weighing them with her eyes. Helgo broke the silence.

"We need a dose of the serum."

"What are you offering?"

"I've got a .38 revolver, some hard rations, and a dope ball."

"I left that behind," Jasmine said.

Helgo reached into a pocket and pulled out Cally's plastic bag. "I picked it up."

Kara nodded at Jasmine."A dose for her and who else?"

"Just her."

She shook her head. "No, you'll be needing two doses."

"Why's that?"

"Because if you're taking Ryan Shaw's sister topside, it's going to upset the delicate peace, which will tumble down tenfold to us below."

Jasmine glanced at Helgo, who slumped a bit at the words.

"What makes you say that?" Jasmine said.

Kara inclined her head and gave a tight smile. "Because before I was exiled here, I was one of the Creator's staunchest supporters on the council. You have his look." She leaned in and sniffed. "You have the same scent of power about you."

"I'm not like him."

Kara remained silent for a moment, considering Jasmine. "That can only work in your favor since the residents topside made it clear they no longer desired a benevolent overlord."

Jasmine's heart lurched. "Is he still alive?" She wasn't sure which answer she wanted.

"Could be. Some say he escaped the coup and fled. Others swear he was captured and his body thrown back to the sands. All anyone can agree on is that he is no longer up there." She said, raising her eyes.

"So we came here for nothing," Jasmine said.

"Someone up there must know the truth," Helgo said.

Kara's lips thinned. "When the mob broke into his chambers, the Creator was already gone. It seemed to me he had been tipped off and had an escape plan in place, or was given one. In either case, he had to trust someone with his life."

"But it wasn't you, was it?" Jasmine said.

"No," Kara said with a shade of vehemence. "While I regret it now, I was the one who led the mob."

"You regret?" Jasmine asked.

"Paradise City is a jewel floating on a cesspit. The Creator kept it supplied with food, water, and power. He welcomed the refugees from the Badlands and organized them. Eventually, he bound part of his power in the rock itself, making Paradise City self-sufficient. The gardens grow food, the larders refill themselves, factories produce the airships and other goods needed to sustain the city.

"Some looked around and realized that, by accident or design, they weren't dependent on the Creator who had retreated from the public eye. One day he decreed that the city was full, and so the Undercity was born. The Creator went into seclusion and left running the city to us on the council. Rumors circulated. Some claimed all his power was bound in the city with none left for himself. Others said he deliberately sabotaged the city to make it more dependent on him. Always there were whispers of perverse acts taking place in his chambers with girls gone missing from the streets or ferried up from the Undercity. Arguments broke out, then fights between those following the Creator and those thinking we could do better."

She clasped her hands and ran a thumb over her knuckles. "We would not follow an impotent god who screamed out in his dreams and awoke pale and shaking, scrubbing his face and hands until his skin wore raw. I could barely look at him anymore and recognize the man who made Paradise City arise from the sands. Then the riots came and I myself opened the gates and joined them."

"If you were part of the coup, why are you down here?" Jasmine asked.

"The aftermath didn't go as I had expected. With our omnipotent

Creator gone, blame fell elsewhere for the city's problems. Some executed, others..." She spread her hands. "Exiled for speaking out, traitors to the revolution. Oh today, there's been a reconciliation between the factions though neither side trusts me anymore."

Helgo gave his black-toothed grin. "So why do we need two doses? Can't take you. Too recognizable," he said.

"I know. You're taking my daughter."

"I'm no baby sitter," Helgo said. "We've got places to go and people to avoid."

"She'll break away once she gets up there. I have friends topside that will take her in."

"Won't the guards recognize her?" Jasmine asked.

"Uh huh," Helgo said. "Seems like extra risk on our part."

Kara shrugged. "If you'd rather stay down here, that's entirely your choice. You can try your luck in securing an opening. I heard one became available this afternoon. Or you can join the permanent population that services the suckers and the desperate."

"All right," Helgo said. "Get us two doses and I'll get your daughter topside."

"I thought you would. Tatiana!" Kara leaned out of the tent and murmured to her daughter. The girl ran away and came back a minute later with a bread roll in each hand and held them out to Jasmine and Helgo.

Jasmine caught her eye as she reached for the roll and smiled. "Thank you, Tatiana. I'm Jasmine and that dirty thing over there is Helgo," she said, jerking her head towards him. The girl remained silent and kept her face blank.

"Eat," Kara said. "I will gather what's needed. Tatiana will mind the door and keep the curious away." Tatiana's eyes rolled to her mother, and she frowned. Kara arched an eyebrow, and the girl left the tent with a slight huff.

"Stay inside," Kara said and left.

After Kara closed the tent flap, Jasmine grabbed Helgo's arm.

"Doses, Helgo? Doses of what?"

"I'm a necro. I can get us a ride up if I'm bringing in trade goods."

"Deaders."

"Right. You see how desperate these people are, how many times do you think someone's tried disguising themselves as a deader? So they have this test. They take a needle as long as my forearm and stick it through the deader. If it screams, then it's not a deader. The serum helps you pass the test."

Jasmine swallowed. "So these doses you're talking about?"

"A cocktail of drugs that block the pain while leaving the person enough upstairs to stumble around. They call it deader serum."

Jasmine's stomach clenched. "No."

"Whatya mean?"

"I mean no. The Caliph's harem master, he..." and her throat closed up as she pushed the memory away. A dizzy, floating feeling, unable to control her own body, helpless as she was led around. Then the Caliph on top of her, then it was Ryan, someone screaming–

"Jasmine," Helgo said. He squeezed her hand and looked at her with concern.

Jasmine slowed her breathing and relaxed her shoulders. "There's got to be some other way."

"I can't think of one."

"Maybe we could wait for an opening."

"The poor sod that got tossed back today? Think his spot's still available? For all we know someone upstairs might have been paid off to *make* that spot available. There are people here who have been waiting for months, a year perhaps. Bribes paid, promises made and broken. How do we fight to the front of that line? We may never get you topside, even assuming we can keep your identity secret."

"Ryan's not even up there," she said. "Let's get what we need down here, leave, and go after him."

Helgo shook his head and placed a hand on her forearm. "We need a ride. An ornithopter at least, though an airship would be better. Supplies, a clue of where to start. All up there, not down here." he said, pointing.

"It's too risky," Jasmine said. "We can figure out something better."

"Yeah, and how long until you get noticed? Or another necro blows through with deaders on a string and they start acting funny around you? Kara already recognized you. There might be others, ones who will sell you out for a chance to go topside."

Jasmine snatched her arm away. What would Cally do? Hadn't she waited in a dilapidated shack waiting for Ryan to come? Jasmine could do that. But no, she thought, when it came down to it, Cally had left when it was a hopeless cause, blowing it all up behind her and never looking back. She did what she had to do. Jasmine would do that.

"Fine," Jasmine muttered. "So long as it works." Outside, Tatiana shifted on her stool. Jasmine leaned closer to Helgo. "What about the daughter? Can we trust her?"

"Lot of anger in her." Helgo spread his hands. "Let's hope she hates living down here more than selling us out."

Jasmine turned the roll in her hand and decided she wasn't hungry. She put the roll in her bag. There. At least she wouldn't go hungry later.

THE SERUM DIDN'T LOOK like much, just a cloudy liquid in a stoppered vial. Kara held two needles as she explained the process.

"It takes a minute for the serum to take effect. First, you will feel a cold stream running down your spine into your bowels. Then the cold turns warm all through your body like a fever. When it seems like you can't take it anymore, it all goes away and you fade into a twilight state. You will feel nothing, like you are not even in your body. Focus on walking. Pay attention to the ground before you step; your feet will be too numb to trust. I also secured this." She held out a makeup case and a dripping bag. "Something for the eyes, and some for the nose. A little carrion will sell our ruse."

"Our ruse?" Jasmine asked.

"Our ruse," Kara repeated, meeting Jasmine's eyes. "I have as great a stake in this as you. Some may say greater."

Jasmine turned to Tatiana. "How do you feel about this?"

The girl gave her a sullen, contemptuous look and held out an arm to her mother, pulling her sleeve back.

As Kara filled the syringe, Jasmine had to stand. Something burned at her wrist and she looked down, catching herself twisting the bracelet into her skin. She stilled the hand and forced herself to watch as Kara approached. The needle plunged into the girl's's arm and Kara brought the plunger down in one slow stroke. Tatiana's hard eyes stayed on Jasmine until her face went slack. She turned to her mother, and a tear fell. Kara held her in her arms until Tatiana sighed. When Kara pulled away, no sign of intelligence remained in her daughter's eyes.

Kara took in a ragged breath and prepared a second needle. Jasmine's heart fluttered, and she had the sudden urge to flee or knock the drugs from Kara's hand. Her breath came in short spurts. She couldn't breathe. Her fingers tingled, and her left arm ached.

"We can wait, Jasmine," Helgo said.

"No we can't," said Kara. "There's not enough left in camp to try this twice."

"No, it's okay," Jasmine said. She turned her head and held out her arm. She felt the pinch, then a push that wormed and twisted its way deep into her core. She shivered for a moment then flushed into a sweat. While part of her panicked, something else swelled in her and embraced the numbness.

Right foot, step. Left foot, step. Jasmine was an awful puppeteer, and she didn't care. She focused on putting one foot in front of the other and leaned into the serum's pleasant numbness. She felt fantastic, even the leather straps tethering her to Helgo couldn't ruin her mood. Tatiana shuffled beside her on her own tether, eyes cast down at her toes. Helgo kept the reins slack for the most part and thankfully people tended to get out of the way when they saw her coming. Or was it the smell? She couldn't feel her nose enough to wrinkle it, yet still caught whiffs of herself with every step. What a funny thing for people to be scared of two skinny girls led along by an equally skinny man humming a song from the Talking Heads. A familiar tune, she could almost place the lyrics. Just on the tip of her tongue...

Jasmine's step faltered, and she stumbled to a knee. She got up, pushing with limbs heavy as wet sand. Focus. Left foot, right foot. After what could have been a few minutes or a few hours, Helgo stopped before the city guard sitting under the umbrella. The ones with pikes didn't quite point their weapons at her, but Jasmine imagined she would get spitted if she made a sudden lurch.

"Name, corpse-spinner?" the sitting guard asked.

"Helgo. And it's 'necrosonic engineer,' if you don't mind."

The man looked past Helgo and grunted at Jasmine and Tatiana swaying behind him. "Lose your ride?"

Helgo shrugged. "Got dropped off to check the traps, found these two, but my airship never showed up. Must have gotten jumped."

The guard gave him a steady look. "Lucky you were close enough to walk it."

Helgo held the stare for a few moments then spat to the side. "Lucky I wasn't on board when the ship got hit. The rest is debatable. You going to let me up top so I can turn in my haul, or what?"

The seated man shrugged and called over his shoulder. "Test 'em."

A guard put his pike down and stepped forward, pulling a long silver spike from his belt.

"Disinfect that," Helgo said. "I have a hard enough time keeping surface rot away, don't need any deep crap."

The guard didn't seem to mind, dumping something like alcohol on the spike and rubbing it with a bandanna. "Hold out their arms."

Helgo glanced back and gave a whistle. Jasmine lifted her arm and watched as the guard grabbed her elbow, pushed back her robe's sleeve, and pinched the back of her arm. She breathed out as the spike entered and pushed through her triceps. Her skin stretched and the spike's point burst through the other side. It was like watching it happen to someone else. Blood trickled down and dripped from her elbow. Jasmine watched it splatter on ground with detached fascination as sand coated each drop and sucked the moisture away. Gnawing pain crept down her arm. Jasmine's head cleared as the wonderful numbness fell away and the wound closed.

The blood, of course. Fixes everything: wounds, disease, poison, even raises the dead if you smear enough around. Grossest Badlands blessing ever. Fortunately her sleeve covered her very un-deader-like healing.

"Wait!"

Jasmine looked up as Helgo was knocked to the ground. The other guard pushed the spike through Tatiana's hand. Her fingers curled as it drove through her palm and with a wet snap one finger went limp. The guard grunted as the spike caught on bone, and he wiggled it around before sending it bursting through the other side. The girl's face never broke, but a small groan escaped. The guard cocked his head.

"Did she say something?" he asked.

Jasmine suppressed a shudder while her heart thudded in her ears. She glanced at the other guard with the pike, wondering if she could grab it from his hands before he skewered her friends. Helgo gave her the minutest expression, telling her to wait.

From the ornithopter, muffled voices. The guard peered into Tatiana's eyes and twisted the spike. Her eyes went glassy and her breath hissed out. Jasmine clenched a fist, then wondered if she shouldn't try kicking the guard's knee sideways instead of hoping for a knock-out. As she gathered herself, Helgo spoke.

"They can feel pain, you know," Helgo said to the guard under the umbrella.

"Bullshit," said the guard with the spike. "Something's not right with this one."

The guard under the umbrella was about to speak when several somethings in the ornithopter began banging against the fuselage. A pilot's head popped up from the deck with a panicked look.

"Sergeant, the deaders are all mumbling and thrashing around in the hold."

"Are they still secure?"

"For now."

Helgo squinted at the ornithopter and leaned closer to the Sergeant. "They've been acting screwy over the past few weeks, hissing and more googley-eyed than normal, right? I can try calming them down if you like."

The sergeant seemed to think about it for a few moments. Blood dripped from the spike in Tatiana's hand.

"Fine, see what you can do. We dust-off in five." The sergeant jerked his head at the guard who sniffed and removed the spike. Helgo flicked his eyes to the ornithopter before humming a tune and gathering the tethers. Jasmine and Tatiana shambled behind him.

∿

In the hold, Helgo strapped her into a slide-out bunk near the floor. Hers was one of a dozen others stacked along the walls, each filled with a hissing, moaning deader rolling it eyes for a glimpse at what it could feel but not understand. Tatiana was in the bunk above, holding her hand awkwardly.

"Helgo, let me heal her at least," she whispered. The necro shook his head as he sang some cotton-candy love tune that could have been from Depeche Mode or Air Supply. It may as well have been Metallica for all the calming effect it had on the deaders.

"Bigger problems, Jas," Helgo said. "You've gotta turn down the wattage on your juju. This close in, it's riling them up."

"But Tatiana–"

"Has to tough it out until we're topside."

A deader in a ripped shirt and jeans with hair somehow still sculpted with mousse pawed at Helgo's shoulder. "You work a healing, it might just send these poor sods into a frenzy and they'll tear us apart or worse." He pushed a mummified hand back to its bunk and re-cinched the deader's straps. "I'll dampen what I can, you try to make yourself invisible."

"How?"

"I don't know, imagine you're a hole in space and time or something."

Fuck. Okay Jas. Relax, ignore the staring dead people. Forget about that girl's blood splattering on the floor. Forget about getting caught. Forget the way you're all tied up and completely vulnerable. Fuck, Fuck, Fuck!

The moaning and thrashing around her grew louder.

Settle. Settle. What would Bishop do? Something calm. Some music. Helgo controls them with it, Ryan was obsessed with it. Think of something calming.

Instead, the chorus to "Our House" popped into her head. The synthy-happy song by Madness that just repeated itself over and over again so even drunks could sing along. As the refrain ran through her mind, the bodies around her settled, some swaying in time to the rhythm. Eventually, the moaning stopped altogether.

Helgo let out a breath and clasped her hand. "That's it, Jas. Keep it up."

"For how long?"

"Until we get to the top, maybe fifteen minutes?"

Jasmine tugged at the restraints. "Then loosen these."

Helgo glanced around. "Okay, don't let them see you moving around."

"I'll cinch them back before we land."

Helgo undid the straps and left the cargo area. Jasmine repeated the chorus in her head and discovered humming worked just as well on the deaders. The ornithopter's engines started, a low growl that soon morphed into a high-pitched whine. When the craft shuddered and lifted into the air, she rolled out onto the floor and stood up. The deaders' eyes followed her but stayed placid as she kept humming. Tatiana, on the other hand, was coming out of her drug haze and starting to panic.

"My hand," she whispered. She fought at the straps, eyes wide and unfocused.

"It'll be okay," Jasmine said. "I'll heal it for you when we're in the city." A deader began moaning, and she quickly went back to humming.

"It *hurts!*"

Jasmine nodded and held a finger to her lips.

"Can't move!" She thrashed against the restraints. Jasmine went to loosen them, then paused. The girl was still slurring her words and might not be able to control herself. Jasmine couldn't possibly keep the deaders calm and mind Tatiana at the same time.

"Lemme out!" Jasmine clamped a hand over Tatiana's mouth and shook her head. *Wait,* she mouthed.

Tatiana glared and bit her. Jasmine snatched her hand away, blood already welling. The deaders began screaming. Tatiana held the small chunk of flesh between her teeth, a feral look crept into her eyes.

"Tatiana, whatever you do–" Jasmine began.

The flesh disappeared with a swallow. She gave a pink-tinged grin then her eyes rolled back and she went limp. The din of the screaming deaders rose even as Jasmine's finger sealed itself and began knitting new flesh. The blood dripping from Tatiana's hand slowed as the wound sealed. Jasmine closed her eyes and concentrated on the words to "Our House," but the deaders kept screaming. She pictured what she remembered from the band's video: boys dressed as lower-class laborers except for fashionable round-rimmed sunglasses, swaying and singing together in a tiny flat. She concentrated harder. The lead singer, whoever he was, dressed in a (for the time) modern jacket, black t-shirt, black fingerless gloves, and a flat-top haircut that shouldn't have worked but somehow did.

The screaming subsided as she kept the video going in her head and sang out loud. In her head, the band danced around, hamming it up for the camera as they sang the same words over and over again. She pictured the video's drab browns and grays which always depressed her despite the cheerful melody. The ornithopter's floor swayed, and she stumbled against a deader's withered leg. At her touch, the former man or woman—she couldn't tell which—caught its breath and quieted. Jasmine reached out to another deader, dressed in neon green shorts and faded red high-top sneakers. In her head, the band paraded around with knotted handkerchiefs on their heads, like a Monty Python skit. The deader quieted.

She went down the row, touching deaders, humming the song's guitar solo. They went down quietly one by one, and she had just rushed back to her own rack as footsteps clanked down the cargo hold ladder. A crewman rushed through, pistol in hand, glancing all around. He stopped at Jasmine's rack, his breath coming out in ragged heaves. So near the floor, she only saw his lower half and the twitching fingers on his free hand. She hummed as quietly as she could, coming now to the song's end. The crewman suddenly squatted, and she shifted her gaze forward. From the corner of her eye, the pistol came down and she sensed the black muzzle hovering at her temple. His hand patted at her stomach, then came a rough tug as he cinched the waist belt, followed by the legs, and hands. Finally, the gun disappeared as a head strap locked her in place. Then he was gone and up the ladder.

Jasmine restarted the song, fighting a gnawing panic as she tested her bonds. The crewman hadn't fully tightened the wrist with Bishop's guitar string bracelet and she moved it back and forth against the restraint as a balm against the urge to thrash against the straps. Above her, Tatiana was quiet and hopefully would stay that way. Her little act of cannibalism had healed the puncture, but would it have other effects?

Jasmine spent the rest of the flight repeating that stupid song and chafing her wrist raw against the guitar string bracelet. Too bad the serum wasn't still in her system, she thought. She would welcome forgetting herself for a little while.

∼

It was all Jasmine could do not to breathe a sigh of relief in front of the crew when Helgo released her. Tatiana moved stiffly beside her as Helgo led them from the cargo area, the girl's eyes even harder than before. Paradise City up close reminded Jas of some Victorian movie set. Dun-colored buildings with round windows set into steep-peaked roofs leaned over cobbled streets that twisted and turned without reason. The people wore suits and dresses that blended 80s punk with Victorian England—ladies wearing ankle-length dresses in neon colors and elbow length fishnet gloves, the men in tweed suit coats and bowler hats also sporting skinny ties and popped collars. Though this style dominated, others wore desert-style robes and head scarves like she had seen in the Caliphate, enough so that her own clothing was not unusual.

The air seemed cooler up here, making Jasmine wish for a coat, the first time since the Badlands. From what Jasmine understood of Victorian London, there would have been smoke and horse dung in the air but here it seemed clean apart from the sickly sweetness of the deaders and her own unwashed body. She wanted a shower. A long, long shower with hot water and honest-to-goodness soap slathering her skin from tips to toes.

Helgo had them shuffle along behind the other deaders toward a weathered warehouse. The other deaders were led away by humming and singing men dressed in black, who cast a wary eye at Helgo as he nudged Tatiana away from the procession and down an alley.

"Problems?" Jasmine said, trying not to move her lips.

"They could tell I wasn't part of their program. Worried I might set off a harmonic or de-synch their rhythm and upset their cargo."

"How could they know?"

Helgo grinned. "Our feet weren't moving to their beat. Ah now–" They turned into a twisting alley and out of sight. Helgo produced a key and unlocked their chains. "Party's over, ladies."

Jasmine rolled her neck and shoulders as the tension left her. As soon as she found a bed, she would sleep for a week.

"So where do we go from here?" she asked Tatiana. "We should get you to your mother's people."

Tatiana nodded as she flexed her hand and rubbed a fingertip over the discolored skin on her palm where the spike had gone through.

"Does it still hurt?" Jasmine asked, unsure if the healing had been completely successful. "You want to talk about what happened?" *You want to explain why you thought eating a piece of me was a good idea? How close are you to becoming a deader, anyway? How close are the others?*

Tatiana startled and dropped her arms to her sides. "It's fine," she said. "We need to go to CBBG Park. There will be someone there who can help."

"I know it," Helgo said. "That's where all the malcontents hang out. Stick close and look like you belong here."

Jasmine couldn't help it, she let out a giggle. "Sorry," she said. "You sure your friend will be there, Tatiana?"

"Said so, didn't I?" she mumbled. She glanced at her hand again and frowned. "We going, or what?"

4

Though no one made any overtly threatening actions, Jasmine felt nothing but hostility and mistrust in the people they passed on the streets. Eyes made brief or no contact. Hands rested near pockets and waistbands or clutched purses with suspicious bulges. Small groups at sidewalk cafes talked with heads close together, laughing too loudly as she walked by. The city militia patrolled in groups of six, marching with exaggerated arm swings and crashing their boots on the cobbles. When they did happen to stop, one guard would accost a citizen loudly for all to hear while the others formed an outward-facing circle with hands on truncheons.

As they passed under the wrought-iron archway of CBBG Park, Jasmine breathed a sigh of relief. There were actually songbirds here, little brown things with blue wings. She had only met crows in the Badlands, mostly around the Love Shack, Cally's deader-proof fortress. For all the problems people here had, at least they lived with songbirds and not crows. She followed Helgo along a crushed gravel path and came upon a small group watching a play. On stage, a man and woman stood on either side of a large picture frame, drawing portraits of each other as they delivered their lines.

"*Take on Me,*" Helgo said.

"Pardon?"

"The play, it's *Take on Me.*"

Jasmine pointed to another group moving to the wings, outlandishly dressed in pointed hats, sunglasses, and polka-dotted suits. "And them?"

"The next show. I don't know it. *Sharp Dressed Man*, maybe?"

"*Fight for Your Right*," Tatiana said.

Jasmine watched as the man stepped through the frame and embraced the woman, eliciting applause from the audience. They took a bow and moved off as the stagehands removed the giant frame and began arranging cream pies on a table. A polka-dotted actor addressed the crowd.

"For your pleasure, the Fourth Ring Acting Troupe will now perform *Fight for Your Right*, also known as *Fight for Your Right to Party*. There will be a brief pause after this performance to clean the stage before we continue with *Safety Dance.*"

"Told ya," Tatiana said.

Did Ryan introduce this himself, or was it something he made the city collectively dream? He was never interested in the theater growing up, but MTV played constantly in the background at their house growing up whether it was homework, doing dishes, or whatever it was he did in his room after school and late at night.

"Let's go," Tatiana said, "This play sucks."

They continued on to a central area featuring a fountain surrounded by white marble statues. Men and women stood around the fountain's lip and harangued small groups passing by. A squad of militia stood to the side, watching the speakers without interest.

"We should be safe here for a bit," Helgo said. "They let anyone spout off on whatever they want here. The goon squad's just in case someone else takes offense and starts a fight."

Tatiana nodded at a man speaking to a small audience. "That's Robin, my mother's friend. You two stay here and I'll arrange an intro, okay?"

Helgo looked to Jasmine, who nodded. Tatiana strode off and worked her way into the audience until she stood in front. If Robin recognized her, it didn't affect his ranting. Jasmine wandered over to the statues, which seemed familiar and out of place in this society.

She approached one of a man arched backwards, playing a v-shaped guitar, smiling in orgasmic bliss. His fingers crowded around the cutout, tapping at the frets. Inscribed on the plinth: SAINT VAN HALEN. On the next plinth the statue wore a top hat low over his eyes and crouched over his guitar: SAINT SLASH. She continued down the row. A wild-maned man holding his guitar before him like a Templar's sword: SAINT YINGWE. A man with long stringy hair and a bandana, body curved in a serpentine shimmy: SAINT AXEL. At the feet of some statues lay the remains of bouquets, candles, and tiny liquor bottles.

"Why do people leave offerings?" Jasmine asked.

"Each of these are supposed to have an affinity for certain aspects of life. The tradition is to make a little offering and whisper your wish."

She stopped before a man holding a headless bat in his clenched fist." Who's this?" Jasmine asked. "The patron saint of exterminators?"

"Saint Ozzy," Helgo said. "Patron saint of travelers."

As they made their way to the far side, Jasmine approached a newer statue, marble still bright and gleaming. A familiar face in aviator sunglasses, Chuck Taylor sneakers, and standing with thumbs hooked into his jean's belt loops: BISHOP THE LANDWEAVER. A wave of sadness washed over her, and Jasmine squeezed her bracelet.

"This wasn't here before," Helgo said. "He helped so many flee the Badlands and find the city."

Jasmine stared at the statue's face, its mouth slightly turned at the corners as if about to make a sarcastic remark. There were no offerings at his feet. "Not a patron saint of anything," she said.

"Your brother was the head of everything, the final word on who was worthy, head of state, or high priest of his own church. Since he left, the council has been unwilling to venture into..." He waved his hand and after a moment shook his head. "I guess their focus is more secular."

"Who runs Ryan's church?"

"There's some debate on that. His high priestess is on the council, but it's said she has had to quash more than a few power plays within the priesthood. Last I heard, there was a new contender preaching revolution down in the farming caverns."

Jasmine lowered her voice. "This city feels like it's going to explode."

Helgo's gaze followed one of the blue-winged birds as it flew from tree to tree. "The airships still leave and return on time. Everyone up here has food, security, light. They worry more about the Caliphate or being cast back to the Undercity. So long as the council can still keep the basics supplied, we should be all right." His eyes narrowed. "Hey."

"What?"

"Where's Tatiana?"

Jasmine glanced where Robin was still speaking, but no Tatiana. A flicker of movement caught her eye.

"There!"

"Stay here," Helgo said. "I'll get her." He ran off, angling to cut off Tatiana's escape. Robin shouted after him and then launched himself from his box, tackling Helgo. As the two wrestled, some bystanders closed in around the two and shouted, others turned and walked briskly away. Jasmine hurried after the girl herself when she bumped into the gray uniform of a militiaman. Hands gripped her arms from behind.

"She's the one," a voice said. "Take her."

Handcuffs pinched her wrists, and she was hauled to a waiting carriage, a kind of paddy wagon. She threw elbows and kicks with panicked strength, eliciting a grunt from one militiaman and a clout behind the ear from another. Her backside hit the carriage floor and the doors slammed shut before she could get to her feet. As the carriage pulled away, Jasmine shouted for Helgo through the carriage's tiny, barred window. The carriage turned a corner, and she glimpsed Tatiana's head darting behind Bishop's statue.

5

The carriage wound its way through the streets to the city center, arriving at a grand building. Atop its blue-tiled dome a statue raised its arm overhead, fist clenched with extended index and pinky fingers, saluting the city with the metal horns. Jasmine didn't need to see the statue close up; it was her brother.

They frog-marched her through marble-floored corridors into a sitting room with large round windows overlooking the city, Persian-style carpets, low-backed leather couches, and several oval-backed chairs upholstered in red velvet. A sidebar held a tray piled with sandwiches, fruits, and a water pitcher.

"What's all this?" she asked.

"You're a guest of the council. They'll answer your questions."

"Do they always arrest their guests, or is that the standard euphemism?" The guard said nothing and bolted the door after closing it. Jasmine crossed the carpet to a single door set on the far side and found it locked as well. The scent of bananas set her stomach rumbling, and with a mental shrug she went to the sidebar and dug into the spread, making sure to pocket a few items for later. The water didn't have even the tiniest bitter of metal aftertaste, and she drank deeply. The sandwiches held cured meat with mustard and the bread had a dense crumb that spoke to an honest-to-goodness bakery somewhere in the city. She ate and paced about, wondering how long she would be kept in the room and what might happen when she needed to pee.

From the window, she watched the city streets. A large crowd approached a park on the city's rim, the people shouting and tossing a white bundle about. When they stopped, a woman climbed onto a statue of some bassist and harangued the crowd. She raised a fist and shouted; the crowd shouted back. She raised a fist again, and the crowd shouted again. She pointed at the council building, and Jasmine shivered as the crowd turned. Did they see her in the window? The crowd roared. Then the woman pointed at a white bundle that Jasmine realized was a bound woman. The woman on the statue swept an arm towards the desert and the crowd charged. They passed the bound woman forward until she was at the very edge, where she disappeared. The crowd quieted, and the woman's screaming curse faded. Seconds later, the crowd gave one last cheer and began dispersing, the majority following the woman who had jumped from the statue and was striding up the main boulevard.

A lock clicked, and Jasmine startled. The single door across the room opened, and a man in black biker leathers and wraparound mirror shades stepped to the side, indicating Jasmine should pass through. Jasmine set her sandwich aside and paused at the threshold. A cold breeze blew past her ankles, and the darkened room of figures beyond radiated the tension of an argument interrupted. Jasmine felt the urge to run.

"The council will see you now," the man in the mirror shades said. He placed a hand on the doorknob behind her.

Jasmine drew in a breath, gave her bracelet a twist, and stepped through.

The room was like a high school gymnasium crossed with a Victorian recital hall, lit only by a dim Moroccan-style lantern hanging from a chain. Jasmine caught half-glimpses of the fresco featuring a cigarette-smoking cherub chatting up an improbably-chested blond angel adjusting her white stockings. The walls displayed paintings of silver airships gallantly fighting swarms of ornithopters and exchanging cannonades with rust-colored zeppelins. Jasmine's slippered feet scuffed against chilled stone as she crossed to a chair set before a long table. Seven figures sat behind the table, each wearing a variation on Michael Jackson's leather jacket from the *Thriller* album over their Victorian dress. She sized up the councilors. Directly before her sat a thin bearded man with a bald pate. His eyes gave no hint of friendliness or hostility as she crossed the floor. Two women sat on either side—a blond whose elaborate hair was held up with a single jeweled pin, the other a diminutive woman in high-collared grey dress who fidgeted with a pen. Both women glanced from her to each other as if asking a silent question. At the left wing sat a woman with gray-streaked hair and classical Greek features who stared at Jasmine with naked hostility. She murmured to a middle-aged man next to her who nodded in agreement. On the right side, a pale man in glasses ignored her completely and doodled on his paper while the bulky dark-skinned man on the end seemed to be watching his fellow councilors as she sat down.

Behind her, the man in mirror shades stomped his foot twice and clapped once in a cadence Jasmine recognized as Queen's "We Will Rock You." He called out in a stentorian voice. "Councilors, the witness has appeared. The chamber is now sealed."

What would Cally do?

She probably would have flipped them all off and sat in the most unladylike way possible. Jasmine wasn't sure it was the best approach, but she'd try it in spirit. She took in a breath to settle her fluttering stomach and clasped her hands in her lap to keep them from fidgeting. She met the bald man's eyes and sat up straight.

"Well?" she said.

The councilman frowned, then gestured to each side of the table. "Miss Jasmine Shaw, recently of the Badlands, we are the Council of Paradise City. I am Augerrie, First Among Equals, to my right are Councilwoman Jordan, Councilwoman Killian, and Councilman Ceder. To my left, Councilwoman Mitchell, Councilman Beecher, and Councilman Ugatu." The two women to each side, Jordan and Mitchell, nodded politely. Killian and Ceder stared holes into her while Beecher absently raised a hand without looking up, and Ugatu turned from his fellows to gaze at her.

"You are here at our request because we know who you are: the sister of our founder, Ryan Shaw. We have been searching for you and find ourselves surprised to find you at our doorstep. How did this come to happen?"

"Happen?" Jasmine let out a small laugh and shook her head. "Isn't this what everyone in the Badlands wants? To get out and join Ryan in Paradise City?"

"That's not an answer," Councilman Ceder snapped.

Jasmine turned. "Okay. I woke up in the Badlands, ran into Bishop, Cally, the Blood Weeper, several hundred deaders, and a few cannibals, got kidnapped, broke out of an airship, and made my way here to find my brother. How's that?"

"Which airship?" Councilwoman Jordan asked.

"The *Caliphate of the Clouds*." Jasmine glanced around. Ceder whispered something to Killian who shook her head, and Ugatu shifted uncomfortably.

"You escaped from the Caliph's city-ship? The impregnable fortress that swallowed a dozen of our best agents? I think not. What deal did you make with him? What price does our betrayal command?"

Mitchell opened her mouth to speak but stopped as Jordan gave a barely perceptible signal to hold off.

"Let's leave the speeches for now and let the witness speak, councilwoman," Augerrie said to Killian. "We are each of us capable of judging her claims." To Jasmine he said, "Forgive Councilwoman Killian's incredulity. Some of us have battled against the Caliph for so long, we have ascribed to him supernatural abilities."

"It's okay," Jasmine said. "Looking back, I find it incredible that—" She was about to say "we," but decided if no one mentioned Helgo, neither would she. No sense in getting him in hot water after all. "That I made it out. Though I suppose with the Caliph's death and his ship on fire, it was easier to escape notice."

The council went still.

"Dead?" Jordan asked.

"That would explain the reports," said Mitchell. "That aerial fur ball in the south—"

"Is classified," shot Ceder as he leaned forward. "Let's not jump to conclusions based merely on what we *want* to hear."

Jordan gave an insincere smile. "The Caliph's death takes the boot off our necks! Let's not discount Miss Shaw's testimony merely because it tells us things some may *not* want to hear,"

"I object to the insinuation—"

Augerrie banged a hammer on a wood block. "Peace, councilors." Jordan's smile remained as she turned it on Jasmine, and Ceder leaned back muttering until Killian whispered something in his ear. "If you please, Miss Shaw. What can you tell us about the Caliph?"

Jasmine found herself twisting the bracelet into her wrist and stopped herself. "Cally, Bishop, and I escaped the Badlands and were captured by the Caliph's men. Cally and I, that is, Bishop died getting us over the gorge."

Augerrie nodded. "A patrol spotted a smoke plume and found Brother Bishop's remains."

"As did the Caliph's men," Jasmine said. "We thought they were city militia, but no." Jasmine let her eyes unfocus. "We were put in his harem —the *hareem,* as the majordomo called it. There, we..." Her voice caught. An oily emotion swirled in her, which she seized in a mental fist and fought down. *No weakness.* "We did what harem girls do. For my part, I was drugged and taken to the Caliph. During our encounter..."

She paused, and it was as if her jaws were wired shut. Should she tell them about Ryan turning into the Caliph? She shifted in her seat and fought against the rising panic in her chest.

How do you think that's going to go, assuming they even believe you? There's a fucking statue of him outside. People pray to him. You're not actually stupid enough to tell them their god raped his sister, are you?

No, no she wasn't. Around the room, some faces softened though Killian's eyes narrowed and she sat straighter.

That one is going to ask for details if you don't say something right now.

Jasmine's words came out in a rush. "The drugs wore off and I drove a hair pin into his brain. Then I set fire to his quarters and made my way out using a hidden passage. When I got to the flight deck, the *Caliphate of the Clouds* was on fire and everyone was panicking. I found Cally, and we ran for an ornithopter. I made it, the Blood Weeper caught her." She took a breath. "My 'thopter crashed and I made my way here."

"The Blood Weeper? Does he still live?"

Jasmine paused. "He was alive when I last saw him on the *Caliphate*. It went down shortly after, but I wouldn't be surprised if he found a way out."

Ugatu grimaced and sat back.

"Was there anyone there who seemed to take charge?" Jordan asked.

"A man in a suit with a shiny pistol, the majordomo, took charge of trying to get the fire under control. He was on the flight deck last I saw."

"Why come here, Miss Shaw?" Mitchel asked. "And why sneak into the city rather than contacting us?"

"I came here to find my brother," Jasmine said. "I thought he would be here, though I now know he's left. As for the sneaking, as you put it, I've found that not everyone had pleasant memories of my brother. It seemed unwise to announce myself."

Killian sniffed. "If you mean that we don't take well to unstable tyrants who keep us weak and dependent on table crumbs." She gave a cold smile. "Yes, you'd do well to be cautious."

"Well said," Ceder said.

Jasmine's face flushed. "I can't claim to know all he did here," Jasmine said. "But I did grow up with Ryan and I heard stories in the Badlands. He has his faults but he doesn't want people to suffer. He's not evil."

Did I just say that? Why am I defending him?

Did she still want to kill him? Now she wasn't sure.

"And we just have to take your word for it, is that right?" Killian spat. She turned to the other councilors. "Despite our history? How he hid behind his so called powers that turned out to be nothing more than flashy parlor tricks when the Caliph's raids began. Or how he locked himself in his rooms and indulged in drink and flesh while the locusts downside swarmed. And here you are, claiming he's not all that bad, perhaps because you want us to think the same of you."

Cally would have punched Killian's lights out.

"I am Ryan's sister," Jasmine said. "I died in my world and woke up in this one, in a building from our childhood. The Badlands is filled with things Ryan knew and cared about. If Bishop and Cally were here, they would tell you how he created everything, how he kept the people alive. He made this world somehow. His influence is everywhere." She stopped as something clicked in her head. "He's still learning how this world works, and while he's learning, he makes mistakes." Like deaders, like the Caliph, like the Cally clones.

"Yes, but why do his mistakes have legs attached?" Augerrie mused.

"And how?" Mitchell said. "For every benefit there is a commensurate penalty to be paid."

"I think he creates without thinking, sometimes in his dreams, perhaps in his nightmares too."

"His inner devil and angel each has a hand on the levers, perhaps. But which hand is heavier?"

"I'm not sure," Jasmine said.

"There is no good, no evil inherent in the creations," Beecher said in a pedantic voice, not looking up from his pen and paper. "There is only how we use them. We need water to live, yet we can drown. The deader in the Badlands kills, but properly secured, it powers our dynamos. I remind you all, we won't have enough food, spare parts, or raw materials to keep the city running for much longer without a source like the Creator. The real question is not whether we survive without him, but can we manage the outcomes if we bring him back?" Faces turned to Jasmine.

"I see a city that promises more than it can deliver. The people in the Undercity resent those up here. The people up here fear each other, whether it's getting cast out or tensions left over from Ryan's departure I can't say." She locked eyes with Augerrie. "I can help you. I'll find Ryan and bring him back, under control."

"Loyalist bullshit!" Killian stood, and the rest of the council erupted with shouts and accusations both at Jasmine and each other. Augerrie eventually got them to quiet down and motioned for Jasmine to continue.

"Ryan and I are twins from a different world. There he died in a car accident. I lived another seventeen years and died on my—our—birthday and woke up in this world in a seventeen-year-old's body. Ryan shaped this world, and he continues shaping it."

"Perhaps if he had been killed during the uprising, his influence would have ended. Instead, it endures as does our suffering," Ceder said.

"Is this suffering, councilor?" Jasmine asked. "The people stranded in the Badlands are suffering. The Undercity is suffering. The Caliphate is suffering. Ryan controls none of it, as far as I can tell. Killing him will not fix your problems." *Though it might make me feel better*, she thought.

Ugatu leaned forward. "We cannot allow him to create another Badlands, or a Caliphate. His power is chaotic creation and destruction, and his mistakes are borne out on our bodies. Would you take his place? Can you do what he does?"

Jasmine let out a breath. "I have some power," she admitted, "I can heal others with a few drops of my blood. Deaders react to me as if they can sense who I am. But I cannot create things as Ryan has. I believe..." she stopped and searched for the words. "I believe I can heal Ryan, whatever his affliction."

She realized she wasn't lying either. Something about it felt right.

"Now that would be worth the risk," Jordan said. "We might finally realize the dream of Paradise City."

"More likely it would shackle us with not one, but two tyrants," Killian said.

Jasmine turned to her. "Was I so hard to find and capture? I need your help as much as you need mine, maybe more so. I have no interest in rule or power, I just want a place where I don't have to look over my shoulder."

"As do we all," Mitchel said.

"Then help me find him so I can heal him. We're two halves of a whole."

"Assuming we agreed, what would you require?" Mitchel asked.

"Ideally, Ryan's location and an airship or small squadron with capable crews."

Ceder pushed back from the table and threw up his hands. "Oh so just a state secret and your own naval fleet then?"

So you do know where he is. Thank you, Councilor Ceder.

"That's enough, councilor." Augerrie stood and pushed his chair back. "I suggest a brief recess to collect our thoughts, then we will reconvene in closed session to consider Miss Shaw's request. Sergeant-at-Arms, please escort our guest to quarters where she will remain available for further questions." He clacked a gavel and the councilors filed from the room. Beecher and Ugatu broke away and came to her.

"What are the chances you'll be able to bring your brother's power under control?"

"Don't ask me to explain it, councilors, but I've experienced his nightmares firsthand." Her wrist burned as she twisted her bracelet. She swallowed and quickly continued. "He showed surprise and regret over what he'd done, which gives me hope. I believe he can change with my help."

Sure, right. If you don't kill him first.

"Be grateful in your certainty, we cannot afford such luxuries. The city will come to ruin all the faster if you fail."

Beecher gave a small shrug. "If the difference between Miss Shaw's success or failure is coming to ruin in a year or a few weeks short of a year, is it really a choice?" He put a hand on Ugatu's shoulder. "But we should discuss this in session. Excuse us, Miss Shaw."

Mirror Shades stepped between Jasmine and the departing councilors and extended a hand. "If you would, this way, Miss Shaw."

6

———————

The bag over her head was musty and scratchy with a tendency to create folds that fell into her mouth. She could do little about it other than blowing or spitting the fabric away. Her shoulders burned from sitting too long in the chair with wrists bound behind her, and her stomach ached from the fists driven into it. The bag was her world, muffling the voices coming from the other room and making them unintelligible and denying her face the cool breeze blowing across her knees and shoulders.

She had spent hours alone in a windowless room while the council deliberated and had fallen asleep in a chair. She startled awake as Mirror Shades knocked and asked her to follow him back into the chambers. One moment she had been following Mirror Shades through a hallway, the next darkness and a gut punch. After that came a quick, muffled fight ending in a bloody gurgle. They lashed her ankles and arms together before she regained her breath. Someone large and strangely perfumed carried her as another set of footsteps echoed, sometimes behind, sometimes ahead. There were stairs, water, and whispers plus reminder thumps to the stomach when she made a noise. Finally, she was dumped and tied to a chair, her captors retreating into another room. A quiet argument started.

She should be scared, she thought. She should be bat-shit raving and thrashing around in her chair, but she felt oddly calm, as if she floated outside herself and watched a skinny girl in desert rags slump in a chair with a dirty black bag on her head. She sat in a large, open space where the sounds echoed. Her feet scraped against a gritty concrete floor. The metal chair squeaked as she shifted weight. She guessed an old warehouse or garage, perhaps a factory.

The murmuring voices stopped. A moment later, a hinge squealed and many footsteps approached. They surrounded her and tore the bag from her head. A large man in brown workman's coveralls and a harlequin mask stood before her. Other figures in identical coveralls and masks stood nearby, men and women both. The man's blue eyes stared. No one spoke. Her eyes adjusted to the light, and she did indeed seem to be in a dirty abandoned warehouse. The air smelled of woodsmoke, and orange lights flickered through grimy windows on the far wall.

What would Cally do?

Jasmine spat lint from her mouth. "Can I help you?"

The large man balled a fist and casually stepped forward. Jasmine tightened her stomach for the gut shot.

"Let it lie," said a woman's voice. The man stepped back.

"Thank you. I don't suppose you could untie me so we can talk like civilized people?" She turned her head as far as she could but couldn't spot the woman.

"I could, but we haven't decided whether the next step is hanging you publicly or throwing you over the side."

"That does put a strain on our relationship," Jasmine said. "Might I suggest you just let me go? I only came here to find an airship."

The woman laughed. "An airship? You really don't know what's going on. Out there, right now, is the revolution. The last remnants of your brother's corrupt government is being dismantled and come morning, we will be in charge. There will be no airships for you."

Oh, so nothing personal, Jasmine, we're just executing you because Ryan's not handy.

No. Give them a reason to keep you around.

"Killing me would be a mistake," Jasmine said. "It starts your regime with bloody hands and lights the fuse for another bloody revolution down the road. Unless you plan on killing everyone who disagrees with you, in which case good luck making that work."

"So says the hidden tyrant," the woman said. "We cannot trust you."

"You don't even know me." Jasmine cast about her brain. "If it's trust you need, ask Kara Moore. She trusted me with sneaking her daughter up here."

"Leave her out of this!" came a familiar voice from her left. Jasmine turned to a masked woman much shorter than the others.

"Your mother trusted me, Tatiana," Jasmine said. "I can't believe she would have wanted this."

Tatiana took off her mask, her young features twisted and narrow. "Mother and her kind live in the past. She's too beaten-down to realize it's time for change."

"So you sold us out."

"You were supposed to be taken to a cell, not the council," said the woman behind her. "Your death at the oppressive regime's hands would have swayed more to our cause but we have enough numbers to win the day regardless."

Eyes flitted between the masked members, one clenched and opened a hand repeatedly. Nervous. Did they even trust each other? "You're not sure," Jasmine guessed.

"It is inevitable," the woman said.

Shadows at the far windows flickered, resolving into figures. The windows shattered. Glass bottles trailing flaming rags tumbled through the air and burst against the floor. The bottles' contents quickly spread as her captors all scattered, some reaching into their coveralls and drawing pistols. A moment later, the puddles caught fire with a muffled *whump*, and the shooting began.

Jasmine couldn't see who her captors were firing at, though soon it didn't matter as the factory floor became obscured in thick black smoke. Jasmine retched and shut her eyes against the stinging fumes. She hopped around in her chair, angling for a nearby table she might be able to smash the chair against or work the ropes at her wrists. Then the chair tipped over. She twisted, sacrificing her shoulder rather than her face. Small hands closed around her throat.

Tatiana. Give her a reason.

"City in danger," Jasmine gasped. "Caliphate—"

Tatiana's knee landed a glancing blow against a kidney. Fingers tightened.

Another reason.

"I healed you" Jasmine said and twisted in the girl's grasp.

Tatiana squeezed. "You tried to make me into one of those *things*. I heard your song and couldn't move!"

Blood drummed in her ears. Her eyes swelled to popping.

What would Cally do?

Whatever it takes. "Your...mother...is..."

The girl's hold slackened. "What?" Tatiana said, coming closer. "My mother is what?"

Jasmine swung her head forward, driving her forehead into the girl's temple. Tatiana's hands opened, and Jasmine sucked in air while stars swam before her. She was partially free of the chair, she realized, and thrashed around until she kicked herself free. Tatiana staggered to her feet and stumbled back. Jasmine rolled and passed her wrists under her feet. She was still bound, but at least she had her arms back.

"Your mother wants you out of this mess," Jasmine said. Who knew, maybe it was even true. Tatiana swung, and Jasmine blocked it easily.. She was bigger and stronger, only hampered by her bonds though those could be useful if she could trap the girl's arm. Hopefully, Tatiana wouldn't pick up a weapon.

But Tatiana backed away, apparently coming to the same idea. She lunged for a table. Jasmine cut her off. The girl circled, then stopped and peeled her lips back into a rictus, making Jasmine pause. Then an arm snaked around her neck and hot metal pressed to her spine.

"Stop," the woman said into her ear. "Tatiana, go check the back door. We're moving to the Fleet Street barricades." Tatiana didn't move, she just stared back with unfocused eyes. "Now, Tatiana," the woman said, with more steel in her voice. Tatiana blinked and a shiver ran though the teen's body as she turned away.

"Your revolution not going well?" Jasmine said.

"Tactical withdrawal," the woman said and pulled Jasmine away from the gun battle.

"Tatiana shouldn't be here," Jasmine said. "She's just a kid."

The woman jerked Jasmine off balance." There are no children here, Miss Shaw, only fighters."

"She's sick. Isn't there something you can do for her?"

"I'd be more worried for your own skin, Miss Shaw. In fact –"

Jasmine's ears popped a second before she was slammed to the concrete. She fought through the closing darkness and ringing ears, willing herself to stand up before her body told her to stay down. Her vision cleared, and she saw Helgo and a tall thin man in a brass-buttoned uniform emerging through a hole in the warehouse wall, followed by several others dressed in leathers and t-shirts. They opened fire on her stunned captors, and Jasmine ran, tripping as she lurched forward. Tatiana and Councilor Killian lay on the floor, eyes staring at nothing.

You need to get away, Jasmine. We can't save the dead.

She turned and sprinted, bullets shattering bricks and ricochets sparkling around her. Helgo's arm waved, urging her on. The motley gunmen parted to let her slip past, and she fell through the still-smoking hole.

Jasmine rolled to the left and came up on hands and knees, lungs heaving. Helgo and the tall uniformed man dashed out, followed by the others, firing back into the warehouse as they retreated. The tall man looked left and right before heading off down the alley with his pistol at the ready.

Helgo grabbed her arm and pulled her up to one knee. He shouted something and tugged harder, bringing her to her feet. Jasmine nodded her thanks and fell in behind him. She wondered if the blast might not have concussed her. One moment she was following the tall man, then she was hunched behind some garbage as those around her traded shots with a group across the street. Then more running, and at least two times she was flat on the ground not remembering how she got there as Helgo shouted in her ear and pulled her to her feet. A building on fire. Twinkling gunfire from wrecked carriages. Pressing flat against walls as militiamen fired from rooftops. A white flower growing in a window box as she hid from an ornithopter's strafing run that chewed through dozens of bodies caught out in the open.

Eventually her brain came back into its own, and she found herself on a flat-roofed tower staring at an airship moored to a slender pole. Like others she had seen, the airship was a long silver cigar shape married to a windowed gondola underneath. Unlike those others, weapon turrets poked out from every angle and the air along its length blurred as if ten thousand silver moths danced around it. The crew wore brass-buttoned uniforms right out of the Sergeant Pepper album; they scurried about, hauling on lines and carrying supplies up gangplanks.

"Almost there, Jas!" Helgo said, his raspy voice somehow cutting through her ringing ears. He pointed to the airship, and she nodded. Behind them, a blue line of lightning flashed then a fireball erupted as an airship one tower over exploded. Bodies fell from the platform, some plummeting to the streets below, others over the side of the city altogether.

"Electro!" Someone shouted and pointed down at a chariot that looked like it had just come from ancient Rome, except it was pulled by deaders rather than horses. One militia guard held the reins while another aimed a gun covered in snake-like coils at the airships. A flare passed between the deaders and raced into the gun's coils which glowed for a moment before another blue bolt shot into the night sky, igniting a passing militia ornithopter.

"They're shooting their own guys," Jasmine said into Helgo's ear.

"We can't tell who's who in this place just by looking. Come on." They sprinted across the platform, Jasmine's skin tingling as she passed through the silver moths. She got halfway up the gangplank when blue light flared; a bolt smeared itself against a barrier yards short of the ship and dissipated.

"Shields?" She asked.

"'Natch," Helgo said with a grin. "Let's hope they hold while we cast off."

The crew pulled up the gangplanks as the last leather-clad rescuer came aboard. The tall thin man pulled a flexible tube from the wall and shouted into its brass-flared end. He then brought the tube to an ear and nodded as a voice shouted back. Somewhere above her, rifles cracked. Mooring cables fell away with pops and clanks and the airship lifted.

PART II

PART II

7

———————

"Helgo, get yourself down to the engine room. Miss Shaw, with me if you please," said the tall thin man.

Jasmine looked to Helgo, who nodded. "This is Mister Chevket, first officer of the *October Sky*, he's one of the good guys. We'll get together soon, I promise, okay?"

Jasmine twisted her bracelet as she examined Chevket. He looked young, maybe nineteen or twenty with pale eyes and curly black hair that covered the tops of his ears. She nodded and fell in behind Chevket, watching Helgo and the others in tattered leathers jog off the other way and down a stairwell.

The *October Sky's* bridge windows overlooked the battle raging in the streets below. The city glowed with orange flames, twinkling gunfire, and the acetic blue flares of deader-powered electros. Two men sat at the very front of the airship where one worked a large spoked metal wheel not unlike a sailboat's, the other man worked a bank of levers and had a similar spoked wheel mounted to his right. Behind them, a stout man with a red-going-gray handlebar mustache and full beard sat in what she assumed was the captain's chair, talking to another man hunched over a small map table with a grease pencil between his teeth.

"I want them thinking we're heading into the Badlands," the captain said. "But as soon as we clear the first marker, plot us a course to the Anvils."

He turned and eyed them as Chevket and Jasmine stepped onto the deck

"This the match that lit the fire, then? Welcome aboard the *October Sky,* Miss Shaw." He tugged at his cannister hat's brim. "Captain Reginald Beaumont, at your service. FAE Augerrie sends his regards. Now if you'll excuse me, I have to get us out in one piece. Chevket!"

"Sir."

Beaumont grimaced as he realized the first officer had slid beside him without his knowing. "We'll come across the city CAP who may or may not fire on us. I'd rather not commit fratricide tonight, so instruct the gunners to aim for disabling shots."

"Sir." Chevket spun on his heel and went to a bank of speaking tubes to relay the orders.

The voices on the bridge were tense but quiet, as was the rest of the ship, the engines made no more noise than a window fan, and no vibrations rattled the airframe as they rose above the city, which made the carnage below all the more surreal. Blue plasma-bolts from ship-mounted electros hummed through the air like ball lightning along with the more familiar pops of small arms fire and low-throated booms of cannon. Sirens wailed as more airships rose from their platforms and fired at the ground, passing ornithopters, even at each other. A half-shadowed airship glowed silver as it shields absorbed an electro-bolt, only to suddenly fail, followed by dark holes appearing in its envelope. Its frame buckled and the ship crashed into a nearby building. As the *October Sky* swung away from the city, Jasmine spied a mob surrounding the blue-domed council building and then *October Sky* turned fully into the darkness, save for the red lights of distant beacons pointing the way back into the Badlands.

Ball lightning shot across the bow.

"Ship sighted," the helmsman said. "Two o'clock high, 2,000 yards."

Chevket took up a pair of binoculars. "Frigate, most likely the *Saxon.*"

Beaumont sniffed. "Skippered by that boot-licker Lawler." A signal lantern flickered from the other ship.

"Well, man?" Beaumont said to Chevket.

"Sir, they're ordering us to stand down and return to port or they will fire."

"Tell them we're under orders from the FAE himself, along with our authentication code."

Chevket unstrapped the signal lantern, a black shuttered box with a long handle, and pointed it at the other ship. He sent out the message, the device clacking loud in the small space as its blinds opened and shut over the spotlight. As they awaited the response, the captain took up a speaking tube.

"Engine room, spin up the dynamos to full power and synchronize shields."

The other craft's lantern began flashing.

"FAE code no longer valid, FAE trying to grow wings. Return to port," Chevket said.

"Grow wings?" Jasmine asked.

"Gave Augerrie a fast trip to the Undercity, over the side," Beaumont said. "Very well, mind the firing instructions, Mister Chevket, and raise shield. Helm, turn us leeward, full revolutions to the engines. Elevator, up 500 feet at five degrees."

The speaking tube whistled, and Chevket bent to answer it. The *October Sky* turned and nosed upwards. The shield's silver moths went frantic as they multiplied until the air around the ship shimmered with a continuous translucent silver bubble. Tinny music drifted from the speaking tube until Chevket stood and replaced it.

"Power systems synchronized, captain. Shield at full," Chevket said.

"Very well, Mister Chevket." Beaumont drew a seat belt across his lap and latched himself into his chair, as did others on the bridge. Jasmine quickly did the same at the map table. Beaumont checked the ship's side-view mirrors which showed the full length of the *October's* envelope glowing orange from lights of Paradise City behind them. From a dark part of the sky, the *Saxon* appeared in reflected blue light as it opened fire. Five spheres of ball lightning grew from pinpricks to the size of small cars as they crossed the distance, flaring and smearing across the shield's surface. As the light faded, so to did the shield, now almost transparent.

"Integrity down to ten percent," Chevket said.

"Return volley."

"Firing." The shield briefly winked out as the ship's guns thrummed, sending ten balls of lightning back at their attacker.

"Elevator, vent cannister seven for a three count," Beaumont said.

The elevator operator acknowledged. "Can seven, vent three, aye." He pulled a lever. The ship sighed and dropped down and to the left. Something whistled overhead.

"You missed!" Beaumont exclaimed and pounded a fist on his chair.

Jasmine followed the *October's* volley. The shots converged and smeared themselves around the *Saxon's* egg-shaped shield, which flared, then winked out. The remaining plasma outlined the airship's envelope in an eerie blue. Then a tongue of flame shot from its side as an engine exploded.

"Their shields are down," Chevket said. "Breaking off."

"Continue evasive action," Beaumont said. "Watch for any 'thopters crazy enough to take on an airship."

The crew murmured "Ayes" and Beaumont relaxed in his chair. For several more minutes, everyone searched the darkness around them for more ships until Paradise City's glow fell far behind them. The captain ordered a stand-down and unbuckled his restraints. "I doubt we'll run into more militia forces tonight, Miss Shaw, though I wonder how long we will escape their notice."

"Thank you for taking me in, captain," Jasmine said, then nodded at Chevket. "And for your rescue, Mister Chevket. I'm not certain I would have been able to escape without your help."

"Think nothing of it," Captain Beaumont said, cutting off his junior. "Just carrying out the council's orders, though that's turned out to be less straightforward now that there may not be a council to report back to."

"So what do we do?" Jasmine asked.

"We continue with the mission. Finding the Creator is our best chance for returning the city back into a properly running machine. With any luck, the remaining loyal members of the council can hold out until he comes back and restores order."

Don't hold your breath.

"I'm not even certain where he is," Jasmine said.

"The FAE provided his last known location," Beaumont said. "We'll lay a trail to throw off any pursuers, then investigate."

"But some of the rebels in the city were on the council themselves. Won't they be able to guess where we're going?"

"Perhaps, but then again, there are bigger problems for the city to worry about."

"The Caliphate," Chevket murmured.

"Just so, Mister Chevket, just so."

8

———————

Jasmine's cabin was little more than a closet with a squeaky bunk. She stared up at faded areas on the ceiling where Chevket's pictures and magazine cutouts had been removed. She didn't feel at all refreshed from the night's sleep. Whether it was a post-serum ache, the abduction, the fighting, or all of it, she just wanted to stay in bed but her stomach disagreed. Her desert robes were filthy with sweat, blood, sand, and industrial-grade grime. Someone in the middle of the night had placed a ship's coverall next to a basin, plus a small towel and a bar of soap. She took the hint. After a quick washcloth bath from the basin, she slid into the stiff garment and pushed the buttons through their holes one by one. The coveralls were too big for her but had one redeeming virtue: large pockets, although she had little to fill them with. She still had the guitar string bracelet, but her accumulated weapons and hoarded rations from the Caliphate and Paradise City were gone, taken by the city militia and her captors in the warehouse.

She stuffed the desert robes in a locker and smoothed out the bed sheets. She rubbed a hand through the stubble on her head and checked herself in a metal mirror. She looked like hell—dark puffy circles under bloodshot eyes and skin hanging loose from her face. Maybe a good strong drink or something from the ship's doctor (if there was one) would take the edge off long enough to feel human again. She rubbed some color back into her cheeks, nodded to herself, and set out into the ship's corridors.

She found the crew's mess by the smell of bacon and the sound of silverware scraping on plates. Rough faces glanced up as she entered. A few wore the same coveralls she did albeit more comfortably and with the odd grease mark or frayed pocket. The other men and women wore the jacketed uniforms with brass buttons and forage caps. The ship's marines, judging by their extra bulk, wore crossed rifle badges on their shoulders and brayed at a table by themselves. Everyone else wore with insignias featuring stylized gears, cannons, or wings and seemed to mix together freely while giving the marines a wide berth. One marine looked up and waved at her and she realized he had been one of Chevket's motley gunmen. She waved back. The last group sat with an empty table between them and the rest of the crew, conspicuous by their lack of uniform and shaggier appearance, if not their more insouciant poses and giving every indication of either falling asleep or on the verge of making a smart-ass remark to their fellows. Among them, Jasmine recognized a familiar face and sat down.

Helgo gave his black-toothed smile. "Jas, meet the engine room crew: Corker, Snot-boy, Jules, Dammit-Hammer, and Yolanda."

The woman blew a stripe of purple hair out of her eye. "Call me Yo."

Helgo nodded. "Engine room, meet Jas. She's a good egg." The rest murmured what passed for "hellos." "Thompson is minding the dynamos right now, you'll meet him later. So, how are you doing this fine morning?"

"Hungry," she said, sitting down next to a dreadlocked kid who nodded along to music he alone could hear. "Anything I need to know before I get in line?"

"You missed chow. The kitchen closed fifteen minutes ago, but here." Helgo pushed his plate across to her, a half sandwich balanced atop a pile of potato chips. "Talk to the captain about getting something more if you need it."

Jasmine reached for the tray but caught herself. "What about you?"

Helgo rattled a pack of cigarettes. "Between these and the cookies I have stashed in the engine room, I'll survive."

"Thanks," Jasmine said and dug into the plate. The sandwich was bland ham spread on tasteless white bread and the chips were a bit gummy, but she ate them, remembering what a feast it would have been in the Badlands.

"Thanks for busting me out, Helgo. I think we're even now." Helgo had been dying in a Caliphate airship's brig and she healed him, whereupon he swore he'd pay her back, a life for a life.

Helgo shook his head. "I'll let you know when we're even."

She felt like she should argue, but held back. Those were civilized thoughts, ideals increasingly worn threadbare as the Badlands taught her survival. She could no longer throw any advantage away, so she weathered the guilty stab to her gut and changed the subject. "How'd you manage finding me?" she asked around a mouthful of sandwich.

"I shook loose from that loony in the park plus two boobs the fuzz left behind after they snatched you, then came to Captain Beaumont and told him what happened. I used to run his engine room, back in the day. He's a little flaky on the surface, but solid underneath. Anyway, he asked around and found you had been with the council and then got snatched. Turns out Chevket knows a guy who knows a guy and after talking about Tatiana's connection, he knew where'd they likely take you. Beaumont ordered the mission and here we are."

"Just like old times, huh boss?" Yo said.

"I'm just here for the ride, and there was an empty seat." Helgo said.

Jules opened an eye. "And the captain gets a necro for free."

"Wasn't enough time to ask for a raise?" Corker asked.

Helgo shrugged and reached over to tug at Jasmine's rolled-up sleeve. "Like the new duds. You want me to find you something else?"

Jasmine fought the urge to glance around and instead focused on a bubbled potato chip. "The clothes are fine, but I do need something. I'm not feeling myself right now, like I'm all knotted together. Is there anything on this ship that'll help with that?"

Helgo remained quiet for a few moments. The kid next to her, (Booger? Mucus?) reached to his breast pocket, but Helgo waved him off.

"There's lots of things on this ship that can get you unknotted, if that's what you want, Jas. Question is, how unknotted?"

"Just enough to take the edge off," Jasmine said. The image of the *hareem* girls sucking at hookah pipes came to her, and she winced. "But not too much," she added.

"I'll see what I can—" His eyes flicked over her shoulder, and he tensed before sinking farther back against the wall and put his boots up on the table.

"Chevket," Helgo said. "How's it hanging?"

"Mister Helgo," Chevket said. "Miss Shaw, my sincerest apologies for not meeting you earlier when you arose. I certainly would have conducted you to the officer's mess, rather than forcing you to eat with the crew, as it were. I am surprised somewhat that our chief engineer has not escorted you himself."

Yo snorted. "Oh Helgo, you done screwed up! He don't want the guests eating with the 'proles." She lifted a pinky and affected an accent. "It just wouldn't do to have her sort with our sort."

"I'm fine, thank you," Jasmine said. "It was good to find a familiar face this morning ."

Chevket's gaze slid from Yolanda to Jasmine."Of course. It would be the captain's pleasure to meet with you at your earliest convenience."

"That means now, toots," Yolanda said.

Chevket looked sidelong at Yolanda. "I am sure there is something that needs attending to in the engine room, Miss Yolanda?"

Yolanda sneered and took in a breath to doubtless launch into a withering tirade, but Helgo cut her off. "It's probably about that time, boyos. Come on down and see us when you get the chance, eh, Jas?"

Jasmine nodded and followed Chevket from the mess hall.

THE CAPTAIN'S stateroom was large enough to squeeze in a table and two chairs but otherwise identical to Jasmine's. She sat across from Beaumont sipping at bitter coffee while the man lifted various piles of books, papers, and odd objects in search of a map that had been there "just a few days ago." The stateroom had a smell Jasmine had always associated with her dad—a mix of sweat, tobacco, and garlic that was nauseating up close but comforting from afar. It seemed steeped into the room's walls and thin carpet. Beaumont himself was no physical specimen—middle-age spread, well-established streaks of gray catching in his red sideburns, and a thinning pate. Despite that, he still radiated a self-assurance that canceled out the otherwise comical search in his desk's chaos. With an "ah" he straightened in his chair and looked over the map that had been mixed in with the cargo manifests.

"This is what we believe to lie at the continent's eastern edge, Miss Shaw." He laid the map between them and tapped a finger at a mountain range. "Our best conjecture is that the Creator established a settlement within the Anvils, which will unfortunately require us to pass over a vast expanse of sand and rock."

"Best conjecture?" Jasmine asked.

Beaumont shrugged. "Our survey ships have not had the best record of returning from that place. There are the usual dangers of weather, Caliphate raiders, mechanical failure and the like, but the *October Sky* was built to survive such encounters. Expeditions to this area have a habit of disappearing without a hint at their fate. Yet there we must go. We know your brother fled in this direction, as had his staunchest supporters. It's rumored that the secret police caught several agents trying to rally others to this new mountaintop utopia."

Jasmine studied Beaumont. Something in his shoulders and set of the eyes leaked through the man's natural confidence. "There's more, isn't there?" Jasmine guessed.

Beaumont blew out his mustache and nodded. "We can hold off any raider attack by the Caliph, and my crew is as solid as they come when it comes to operating in the wastes. Though you wouldn't of course know, we have more than a little experience approaching hostile areas with stealth and guile, which was a strong reason for Augerrie to give this mission to *October Sky*. Another being that other airships capable of this mission are assigned elsewhere. My concern is what manner of harassment Paradise City's usurpers will take. Those other ships could be recalled and tasked with hunting us down, which I believe they will do. In short, I fear my own navy."

"I thought we lost them in the night."

"Perhaps we did, but the usurpers certainly know of your mission and if they cannot guess where we are now, it is not hard to determine where we will go. Certainly this mission triggered your abduction and sparked the uprising, so it seems reasonable they'll try stopping us."

Jasmine sipped at her coffee. "I agree. What can I do to help?"

Beaumont leaned forward. "Be prepared, Miss Shaw. I will do my utmost to get you to your brother but you must convince him to return to the city and restore order. The longer we take, the greater the chance we will be discovered by a force we cannot outrun, outmaneuver, or overcome with force of arms. When that happens, all will be lost."

But what if I kill Ryan when I find him? Would you still help me if you knew, captain?

"That said, I should encourage you to remain in your stateroom and recover from your long ordeal. I will send Chevket to collect you for meals in the officer's mess, or otherwise escort you about the ship if you should feel the need to stretch your legs."

Jasmine set her coffee down. "You're confining me to quarters, Captain Beaumont?"

He held up his hands. "No, Miss Shaw, nothing of the sort. You are of course free to move about the ship, but I would rather you not do so without escort. For your safety and for the...efficiency of the crew's operations."

"You mean don't get underfoot."

His mustache shifted with a tiny smile. "Just so. I'm sure you're a capable woman in your own right, but you've no experience on an airship crew, yes?"

"True."

"Then please do me the courtesy of not wandering about alone especially outside the ship's common areas. In return, I promise you free access to my ship."

"Deal," she said.

"Excellent. I'll call for Chevket to take you wherever you want to go."

Chevket strode before her, ramrod-straight with hands clasped behind his back. Crewmen glanced his way as they approached, conversations ending and crewmen scattering with newfound duties elsewhere. The exceptions to this behavior were the ship's marines, who casually saluted as they passed.

"Are the marines always armed?" Jasmine asked.

"At all times, Miss Shaw," he said without turning. "We are operating in hostile lands and must be ready to repel attacks at a moment's notice."

"That's what the ship's cannons are for, aren't they?"

Chevket stopped at a hatch and stood to the side, gesturing for her to enter with an outstretched hand. "Indeed, Miss Shaw. Though we must also guard against the possibility that there are internal security matters requiring swift responses."

"Internal security? Like boarding parties, armed stowaways, and such?"

"Just so. Also the new possibility of sympathizers among the crew to the usurpers or the Caliphate itself. We must guard against sabotage and clandestine signals."

Jasmine felt like laughing and crying at the same time. "So we're not even safe from ourselves?"

Chevket gave her a small smile. "A precaution only. Prepare for the worst, hope for the best and all that." He looked up and the smile faded until his face was back to its normal state of bland disapproval. "Are you quite sure you want to visit here, Miss Shaw? The engine room is such a loud and—how should I put it—odoriferous section. One wonders how they can stand it in there twelve hours a day every day."

"I don't mind, thank you, Mister Chevket." Jasmine allowed the man to open a second hatch for her and she stepped through, where her senses were immediately assaulted by a low thrumming like fat bees trapped behind her skull, the smell of unwashed bodies, and the subtle sweetness of decay. She headed for Helgo, who shouted and made odd gestures with his fingers at Yo, who stood by a bank of gauges, levers, and wheels.

"And figure out a way to match the impedances at both ends, I'm getting noise from a fifth-order harmonic!"

Yo nodded and turned to study her dials. Helgo noticed Jasmine and grabbed her shoulder.

"Jas! Good to see you." His black-toothed smile relaxed some tension in her neck that she hadn't known she was carrying.

"Mind if I take a tour?" she asked.

"I'm sure they can spare me for a few minutes," Helgo said. He looked over her shoulder and curled his lip. "And you brought Chevket too." He gave a flourishing bow. "It's a signal honor, sir." Someone in the corner went into a coughing fit, and Yo suddenly turned away with quaking shoulders. Chevket stood straighter.

"Notwithstanding your regards, Mister Helgo, the captain would like Miss Shaw escorted by senior crewmen or officers when she is going about the ship and I must supervise a gunnery drill in ten minutes. May I discharge her to your care?"

"Yeah, sure. I'll make sure she's back in time for dinner."

Chevket's heels clicked as he nodded and quickly left.

"He's not a bad sort, but I think he gets the creeps around the deaders," Helgo said.

"Maybe it's that stick up his ass," Snot-boy called out from an overhead catwalk.

"It doesn't help," Helgo agreed. "Anyway, Jas, welcome to the heart of the *October Sky*. Come along with me and mind the deaders. They're mostly shielded, but let's not risk it by you coming too close."

The engine room was smaller than the one she had rescued Helgo from on the Caliph's floating palace, but the layout was more or less the same. In the center stood the ship's dynamo—a donut-shaped sculpture of metal, piping, cabling, and sarcophagus-shaped cylinders containing deaders spinning like rotisserie chickens. Helgo's crew monitored the ship's systems and supervised the process of changing out deaders, swapping sarcophagi from the off-going shift with "fresh" deaders from nearby racks using a small gantry. They also fed and cared for the deaders, feeding them chopped meat and vegetable paste with what looked like extra-long turkey basters and kept them docile with various 80s music compilations and custom concoctions of white, pink, and occasionally something Helgo called "cosmic" noise. The necros filled time between tasks gossiping, playing cards, or more often, playing instruments. A stage stood to the side with a full drum kit, guitars, bass, keyboard, and microphones plus a soundboard that Helgo explained could plug into the deader's feeds when the necros needed to run diagnostics or test a deader's response to various songs.

"You could just slap two deaders in the harness and let them pull," Helgo said. "But it's better if you match their audio response so their output doesn't get out of balance. Fatigues them faster."

"Like the one in our ornithopter."

Helgo nodded. "Like that. Once that happens, they're useless for our purposes."

"What happens then?"

Helgo whistled like a falling bomb and clapped his hands. "We run black noise through their ears and eject 'em. If the sonics don't kill them, the fall will."

"That's not right."

Helgo held up a finger. "It's not efficient. That's why we run 'em in shifts and keep care of 'em, so they last longer. More or less indefinitely unless something else goes wrong."

"Like what?"

Helgo shrugged. "Power surges, battle damage, and good ol' bad luck."

Jasmine and Helgo watched the deaders spin in their sarcophagus pods. The deaders looked docile enough to Jasmine, almost peaceful compared to those in the Badlands that had shambled and moaned after her. She rubbed at her forearm and leaned in.

"Helgo, is there any of that serum stuff on board?"

Helgo gave her a look. "And why would you be wanting any of that?"

She crossed her arms and rubbed at a grease spot with her boot. "I don't. Not really."

His hand reached for her, then stopped as he seemed to think better of it. "There's no call for serum on the ship," he said in a low voice. "But that doesn't mean there's none to be had. If you're really hurting..."

Jasmine nodded. "I'm hurting."

"I'll ask around. But only because I owe you."

"Fine." She tried smiling. "It's fine if you can't find any, I mean. Maybe I only need to stay busy. You have anything I can do?"

"Can't have you too close to the deaders or you'll cause all kinds of interference." Helgo said, then he brightened. "Actually, I need to overhaul the power feeds on this tub. You can help me with that."

While Helgo went off to gather his tools, Jasmine watched the spinning deaders and a wave of wrongness washed over her. Her body didn't seem to be her own, like her flesh was a size too small. She wanted to be numb.

You're not really hurting, you only think *you are.*

Jasmine told herself to shut up.

9

"More slack" came Helgo's echoing voice. Jasmine pulled more coils from the wire spool and shoved them into the shield generator's crawlspace. The generator itself looked like a 1950s console television sprouting a metal tree whose limbs wound between the hundreds of helium gas sacs that filled the cavernous space, spreading upwards and outwards until branching tips met the metal frame supporting the outer skin of the *October Sky's* envelope. Below, a single spike pierced through to the lowest deck and completed the circuit, or so she pieced together from Helgo's ramblings on how the ship's systems worked. The power feeds were among the largest on the ship—two cables as big around as her arm—which fed into the unit's back. The front sported several knobs and dials, which Helgo reminded her several times not to touch, bump, or breathe on, and a screen displayed a ghostly oval that grew and compressed as Helgo swapped out cables and made adjustments.

She sighed and watched the endless sea of dunes, scrub, and occasional drain-swirl cloud. Five days had passed, and her body still ached. She spent most of her time with Helgo or with the captain and wondered if she had made a mistake. The crew seemed overly formal around her, and on those occasions where she tried visiting the crew's mess rather than the officer's, conversations died and she felt their stares on the back of her neck until she left. Maybe they blamed her for the trouble at home, or for Chevket and his marines patrolling the corridors and scrutinizing every task. Or maybe because she hung out with the necros, who the crew called corpse-spinners behind their backs.

It wasn't all bad through. She slowly got her bearings. She even learned the basics of flying an ornithopter when Helgo had to take the ship's launch for exterior inspections, though Helgo still had to take over when it came to docking in the *October Sky's* cramped launch bay.

She stuck a hand into her pocket, bringing out a biscuit she had saved from breakfast and gnawed on it in hopes of distracting herself. A muffled clang made her jump, and a cursing Helgo crawled out from the floor, holding his head.

"Whoever designed that so-called access should be shot in the gut and tossed over the side," he said.

"I'm sure your sacrifice will be worth it in the end," Jasmine said.

He snorted and walked over to the wire spool, grabbing a box and fishing out the parts he needed for assembling a plug. "May be at that," he said. "Either someone didn't notice or skimped out entirely on the wiring when they upgraded the shield. They're lucky the shield hasn't fizzled or blown up under a heavy load." He cut the cable from its spool and began stripping individual wires.

"But we're safe now?" Jasmine asked around another bite of biscuit.

"Safer. There's only so much I can inspect and replace when we're underway."

"The crew hates me."

Helgo shrugged. "My guys seem to like you well enough."

"The crew hates your lot too."

"Hate is a strong word. Pass me some grommets."

Jasmine shook out the metal caps from a box into her hand and passed them over. "What if one of them is working for the other side?"

"Not my guys." He stopped for a moment to think, then shook his head. "The others are probably okay too. Maybe some sympathies, but the captain wouldn't keep someone on board he didn't trust."

A whistle sounded from a grate on the wall followed by Chevket's voice. "*Battle stations! All hands! Battle stations!*"

Helgo swore and began to work faster. The speaker whistled again, and the captain's voice sounded.

"Where are my shields, Mister Helgo?"

"You tell him five minutes or less."

Jasmine pulled the speaking tube and relayed the message to the bridge.

"Miss Shaw, what in blazes are you doing there? Take shelter in your quarters!"

Jasmine arched an eyebrow at Helgo, who chucked his head. "Go. This is a one-person job."

Jasmine made it through the hatch and into the corridor when the cannonade began—deafening booms that shook the airship and set it swaying. She steadied herself and made for a ladderway. Her hands fumbled at the railing, and her foot slipped twice on the tread before she finally settled herself and bounded down to the next level. Crewmen hurried past her with grim looks, unflinching as the next cannon salvo erupted. She caught the drone of ornithopters and the chattering of machine guns, whose bullets rattled like pebbles on a tin roof as they hit the *October's* envelope.

Jasmine rounded the corner onto her room's hallway, pressing herself against the wall as two marines ran the other way. A burst of gunfire ripped through, catching the marines just outside her door. She rushed to them, one man dead already, the other bleeding and struggling to rise. Blood pooled under them both, and bright arterial spray splattered the wall as the wounded man twisted and fell. She knelt beside him and pressed a hand to his leg. The man hissed and looked down, eyes widening, breaths rapid and shallow.

"It's okay," Jasmine said in a voice calmer than she felt. "What's your name?"

The man just stared at the blood seeping out from her fingers and slapped a hand over hers. Jasmine repeated herself.

"Rollins," the man said.

"Okay, Rollins. Don't look down, look at me, okay?"

Rollins's eyes rolled to her face, unfocused.

Jasmine searched around for something to use as a tourniquet but instead her eyes stopped on Rollins's knife. She pulled it free from its scabbard, and without giving herself time to think, pressed her other, blood-slicked thumb to its edge, then into Rollins's leg, willing the bleeding to stop.

Rollins's head rolled back.

"No, no, no. Don't you dare die on me. I'm the goddamn goddess of healing, Rollins!"

His leg warmed, and the bleeding slowed. She couldn't tell if that was a good sign or not, there seemed to be enough blood on the floor to fill a kiddie pool. He stopped breathing.

She shook him. "Rollins, I command you to live."

Nothing.

Failed again, Jas.

"Dammit!" She searched for a tourniquet again, a first aid kit on the wall, anything.

Why weren't you prepared?

Rollins shuddered and gasped. His eyes flew open, and he sat up as if jerked by a cord. Looking down, he wiped at his bloody leg's new flesh where the hole had been. The floor shook, and the sounds of battle returned as Jasmine's focus evaporated. The ship's guns loosed another salvo and the air reeked of burning powder, metal, and blood.

"Ryan be praised," Rollins murmured. "I thought I was done for." Confusion and awe mixed in his eyes. "It's true what they say, isn't it? You're his sister."

Jasmine nodded. "Sorry."

"I thought it was just propaganda. Don't be sorry, I mean, thank you." He turned to the other man's mangled body and frowned. "We need to move."

Rollins pushed himself from the floor, standing with Jasmine's help.

"The captain told me to stay in my room," Jasmine said.

Rollins shook his head. "That burst we caught went completely through your quarters. It's not safe. I was on my way to my station outside the bridge. I'll take you there. It's armored."

Jasmine took one look at the bullet-riddled door and agreed.

"Let's go," she said. She helped steady Rollins and supported him as they ran through the hatchways. Jasmine realized she didn't have anything to fend off boarders. Her eyes locked on the pistol hanging from Rollins's hip.

"I need a weapon," she said.

"I can't issue you one," Rollins said. "Only Chevket or the captain can. Don't worry, we're nearly there."

"Rollins, can you do me another favor then?"

"Yes?"

"Let's keep this healing to ourselves, okay? Especially the goddess of healing part. I don't want the crew any more weirded out than they are already."

Rollins thought for a moment. "All right, but I don't know how I'm going to explain all this blood and the holes in my uniform if someone asks. And they will."

"You helped that other crewman out as best you could." She realized they had just left the man there. "I'm sorry, I didn't even know his name."

"Howe. Terrible at cards, the poor bastard."

"He was already dead when I got to him."

He nodded. "I understand, Miss Shaw, thank you. I'll keep your secret."

They made it to the bridge, Rollins waving her off and continuing on to his post without even a limp.

On the bridge, the captain swiveled in his chair to glare at her but kept up his litany of commands as Chevket and the others rushed to obey.

"Dorsal and ventral guns switch to flack, firing pattern Beta. All other guns continue anti-'thopter and free-fire. Helm, evasive plan Foxtrot."

A crewman acknowledged, but Beaumont was already turning to Chevket.

"Where are my shields?"

"Mister Helgo reports nearly there."

"Would he have the enemy patiently wait until we are ready?"

As if on cue, the air outside shimmered.

Beaumont grinned. "By Saint Willy's beard, it's our fight now!"

A dusky dragonfly shape with a gun sticking from its mouth raced by the windows. Close enough for Jasmine to make out the pilot's desert robes, stubbly beard, and darkened goggles. The 'thopter grazed the shield, and when her eyes recovered from the flare, she spotted it tumbling away with a missing wing.

"Four bandits remaining, coming around to six o'clock high," Chevket reported.

The rear-view mirrors slowly tilted as a crewman tried keeping the action in view.

"They'll have to repeatedly hit the same spot on the shield to get through, Miss Shaw," Beaumont said. "That requirement will restrict their maneuvering options considerably."

The floor shuddered as cannons fired and black clouds appeared between the 'thopters and the ship. Light twinkled from four approaching 'thopters, the shield glowing moments later. The cannons chug-chugged in continuous fire and the 'thopters scattered. Two disintegrated as the *October's* rounds found them. Another evaded only to fly into a black cloud and come tumbling out the other side. The last 'thopter dipped and darted through the deadly airspace until it nosed over and pulled away faster than the *October's* guns could track.

"Last bandit disengaging," Chevket said.

"Very well. He's probably gone for good, but remain at battle stations for now. Compile a damage report and convey my compliments to the gunnery crew, Chevket."

"Sir." Chevket left the bridge, summoning two other crewmen along with him.

Beaumont turned to Jasmine, eyes fixing on her bloodstained clothing.

"Not mine," she said.

"I did direct you to your quarters, did I not, Miss Shaw?"

Jasmine met his gaze. "It was in the process of being shot to hell as I arrived."

Beaumont's eyebrows raised, and he nodded with pursed lips. "In that case, may I say you exercised excellent judgment."

"I want a gun too."

Beaumont coughed. "We're not under attack right now, Miss Shaw. All weapons will be stowed shortly."

"What if we're attacked again?"

Beaumont's face became pinched and red. "Then I will determine if it's appropriate for you to have a weapon aboard my ship!" His face relaxed. "I have to think about everyone's safety, Miss Shaw. There are good reasons behind the rules." He held up both hands as Jasmine prepared to light into him. "I have no intention of leaving you defenseless if we're boarded but now is not the time. Let us discuss this later?"

Jasmine swallowed her anger, seeing the bridge crew shift nervously at their stations. "Very well, captain. At dinner tonight?"

"Agreed."

10

———

Jasmine moved through the ship, avoiding the damage control parties. Outside her door, the dead marine, Howe, had already been removed and a crewman mopped at the blood.

"We'll have your room put back to rights soon, miss," he said.

The scene hadn't made her queasy at the time, but now her gorge rose. She fidgeted with her bracelets and tried planning a path around the spill without actually looking at it.

"I'm sorry about Howe," she said.

The crewman shrugged and plunged the mop into a bucket. "Unlucky, that. Nobody else got even a scratch. Still, at least it looked quick."

"It was," she said, regretting it as the crewman's head jerked up. He pointed at the bullet-riddled door.

"You were in there? Ryan's grace, you were lucky."

"No, I was just returning when it happened. If I hadn't stopped to let Howe pass, it might have been me."

The crewman shook his head and slapped the mop to the deck. "Like I said, lucky."

Jasmine's stomach flipped and sweat broke on her brow. She sidled past, pushing her door open.

The wall's jagged holes whistled in the *October Sky's* slipstream, and it still reeked of scorched metal. Her mattress lay on the floor, wadding poking out from great gashes and spilling onto wadded bed sheets. The footlocker lay upside down in the corner, her desert robes and emergency cache of breads, crackers, and cheese scattered and mashed under bloody bootprints. Her stomach convulsed, and she heaved into a wastebasket.

"You all right in there, miss?" came the crewman's voice through the door.

"Yes." She hugged herself to stop the shaking.

She stared at the chaos, mind churning until a single thought brought her back to herself.

What would Cally do? Set traps. Find a weapon. Make those dumb sumbitches sorry.

The trembling faded, and she gave her bracelet a twist.

Right.

She put the mattress against the door so nobody could peek through the bullet holes and cleaned until the mess passed for battle damage. The food had been going stale and funky anyway. She would make sure from now on to eat the fresher stuff and save the rest. She jumped when someone knocked at the door, and she cursed. She shifted the mattress aside and opened the door to Chevket and two other crewmen.

Chevket surveyed the room in a moment and frowned.

"Hinze, patch that wall. Felker, procure a new mattress or failing that, stitch this one back together." Once the men were moving, he asked Jasmine to step into the hall.

The bloodstain was gone with only a faint outline against the deck's dull gray.

Chevket leaned in, speaking with a lowered voice. "Are you in danger, Miss Shaw?"

Jasmine paused. Was he being deliberately intimidating? She balled a fist and tried to breathe normally. "This attack shows we're all in danger, Mister Chevket."

"That mattress was slashed with a knife, not riddled with bullets. Your footlocker was unsecured from its mountings but otherwise undamaged. Unless you did that yourself?" His voice didn't hold accusation, just concern.

Could she trust him?

He did rescue you from the warehouse.

"It was worse before you got here," she said. "Someone had been through my room, either looking for something, or trying to scare me."

She watched his eyes, but she couldn't tell if the news affected him.

"I believe you. There was always a possibility of a traitor aboard, either sympathetic to the rebels or to the Caliphate. I had hoped this wasn't the case, but the captain and I increased security nevertheless." He tapped his chin. "Interesting that our saboteur waited until the marines were occupied."

"You think the attack was a diversion?"

Chevket inclined his head. "If it wasn't coordinated, it was very convenient for his purposes."

"What purposes?"

"Who can know? What do you have that someone would risk this?" He shook his head. "No, don't tell me. Confide in the captain, there's none more honorable. He has a safe in his quarters I'm sure he would allow you to use."

But I don't have anything worth locking up, do I?

Hinze emerged, reporting the patching complete. Chevket sent him off searching for a door.

"I'll assign a security detachment to watch you and station themselves outside your room when you retire for the night."

"Can you be sure one of them isn't the traitor?"

He stiffened. "I wouldn't believe it possible. I've picked many of them myself and they've served with distinction for many tours."

Jasmine raised an eyebrow. "But?"

"While the captain would not agree, I cannot rule out the possibility."

"Then no bodyguards. In fact, I don't want any extra attention—let whoever did this think they got away with it and we'll wait for them to make a mistake. And I want a gun."

A ghost of a smile crossed his lips.

"Prudent. We'll need the captain's blessing, but I think it can be done. Whatever you do, do not suggest one of his crewmen is corrupt without evidence. He would react...poorly."

"We should keep this between us until we have something for the captain."

Chevket checked over his shoulder again. "It goes without saying, Miss Shaw. I am your man in this." He didn't click his heels before leaving but she could tell he wanted to.

Yeah, Jas, but can you trust him?

Too late probably.

11

Dinner was an informal affair in the officer's mess, most drifting in to grab a few items before heading back to their stations. Jasmine balanced a plate on her lap as Beaumont scanned several charts laid out on the table. Jasmine found the Badlands, ringed by a dotted line marking Paradise City's orbit. Two charts over, the markings grew sparse until they vanished behind the notation *Caliphate of the Clouds*. Beaumont's eyes constantly scanned the various charts, always coming back to a particular spot on a coastline labeled *The Maw*.

"Is that where we're headed?" Jasmine asked.

Beaumont blinked and his eyes re-focused. "Near there, I should think. We should be able to spot a city once we get closer to the Anvils. If our luck holds, we will be within the bosom of their defenses before any pursuer arrives."

Jasmine gnawed on a bread heel, sneaking another piece up her sleeve. "How much luck do we need?"

Beaumont blew out his mustache and gathered some condiments from the sidebar.

"This is us," he said, placing the sugar dish mid-way from Paradise City to The Maw.

"The 'thopters we ran into this afternoon were Caliphate raiders, likely from a forward base near here." He placed a pepper shaker on a spot with red lettering. Then he placed a salt shaker behind the sugar dish. "That's my best guess for a city fleet, assuming they saw through our ruse."

To Jasmine's eye, the *October Sky* was penned in on both sides, though still had plenty of maneuvering room. She said as much.

"True, but if we assume the fleet commander knows where we are heading, he will attempt cutting us off."

"And if *he* doesn't?" She arched an eyebrow, but Beaumont wasn't paying attention.

"Then we need not worry, for he will miss us entirely." He slid the sugar bowl forward, then each shaker on an angle until all three touched. "This is the pinch point, Miss Shaw. We must take this narrow corridor between our pursuers and hope we pass undetected."

Jasmine twisted her bracelet and looked over the charts. She picked up the sugar bowl and "flew" it across the charts while Beaumont picked at his plate. Each alternate route she picked came up against mountains too high for the *October Sky* to fly over or else gave their pursuers a greater chance of overtaking them.

A clatter behind made her drop the dish, scattering sugar across the whole table. An officer apologized, picking up his plate and a knife.

Jasmine pictured the knife plunging into her kidneys. Why hadn't she sat against the wall?

"Saint Willy's beard, Mister Tiller, are you in a habit of startling my dinner guests?"

"Sorry, Captain."

Beaumont grunted and lifted the charts, funneling the spilled sugar back into the bowl. Jasmine did likewise as she composed herself. Chevket entered the room, smoothly changing course from the food to the table and assisting with the sugar cleanup. He caught Jasmine's eye and then glanced at Beaumont.

Jasmine gave her chart a final shake and set it to the side. "Captain, we need to talk about a weapon," she said.

Beaumont pressed his knuckles to the table. "Miss Shaw, my crew and I are pledged to keep you safe aboard my airship are we not, Mister Chevket?"

"As safe as can be, sir," Chevket agreed. He paused, as if in thought.

"What is it, man?" Beaumont said.

"Well, sir, today's events demonstrated a blind spot in our assumptions."

"Blind spot? Where?"

Chevket snapped his chart clean. "Miss Shaw's quarters were hit by a stray burst, quarters assumed safe only because we expect functioning shields. Likewise, we assume she doesn't require a sidearm because we expect any boarders will be dealt with by marines and the crew, who also draw sidearms for such actions. Miss Shaw is not crew and therefore, not authorized. Everyone would be armed except Miss Shaw, leaving her vulnerable."

"We train the crew to properly handle their sidearms." Beaumont turned to Jasmine.

"I've defended myself and others in the Badlands, captain. I can handle a gun."

Beaumont pursed his lips and drummed his fingers on his paunch. "Very well, Chevket, you made your point. I'll authorize a sidearm if we're repelling boarders."

"Very good, captain, though if I may continue?"

Beaumont looked puzzled. "Yes?"

"In the chaos of the moment, crewmen and marines fall back on drill and may fail to remember the directive. Moreover, Miss Shaw is not familiar with boarding drills and where the sidearm caches are located. I suggest something more proactive: issue her a weapon for the mission's duration."

"That would be...most unusual. Though I suppose Miss Shaw is a most unusual passenger and these are most unusual circumstances." He stroked his beard. "Very well, Chevket. Please see to it."

Chevket nodded with a little bow. "Yes, captain. Immediately. Miss Shaw." He gave her a little bow and left.

"Unusual times indeed when Chevket decides to bend the rules, Miss Shaw. I never thought I'd see the day." He chuckled. "There is still hope for the man."

He gestured back to the table, inviting her to sit. "A glass of wine while we wait, perhaps?"

Jasmine sat, angling herself to watch the door. The captain poured two small glasses of a pale ruby wine, an overly sweet strawberry concoction she hadn't tasted since a college house party, but did the trick of easing the tension in her shoulders. Even bad wine was better than no wine at all.

"All just preparing for the worst and hoping for the best, really," Beaumont said. "The real test will be how we will be received by the Creator, your brother. With your help, I am confident his wisdom will heal and guide us through the rebuilding."

Jasmine swirled her wine and tipped the glass back. The stuff went down easier in larger gulps. "I hope so, captain."

She thought about confiding in Beaumont but decided involving Chevket was risky enough. She had to find the traitor before they landed.

Chevket returned with a pistol and short-barreled shotgun. "I secured these weapons for you, Miss Shaw, not knowing which would be more suitable."

Jasmine nodded at the shotgun. "I've used one of those before but never fired a pistol."

Chevket gave his not-quite-a-bow, working the action to show the chamber wasn't loaded before handing her the shotgun. "This would have been my recommendation regardless, Miss Shaw. A fine weapon in boarding actions." He handed her a satchel containing a box of shells.

Jasmine took a shell out and began loading.

Beaumont squirmed in his chair. "Are you quite sure it is necessary to do that right now, Miss Shaw?"

Jasmine slid the action home. "Don't worry, captain. I won't go around blowing holes in your airship by accident."

"How comforting," he replied. "If you'll excuse us, Miss Shaw, Mister Chevket and I have some matters to discuss."

Jasmine rose, hooking the satchel over her shoulder and hefting the shotgun. Beaumont opened a ledger book and pointed out an entry to Chevket. As Jasmine passed the sideboard, she checked to make sure the men were still occupied and grabbed the wine bottle. In the passageway, she slid the bottle into the satchel and continued on, mindful of the shadows and listening for approaching footsteps.

~

THE NEXT MORNING, tiny hands squeezed her eyeballs from inside her skull. She skipped breakfast with Beaumont and made a quick dash into the crew's mess to grab a biscuit and coffee. The crew seemed even more unfriendly, some frowning at the shotgun slung over her shoulder. She almost bowled Rollins over as she left.

"Miss Shaw!' he said smiling.

"Mister Rollins. How are you feeling?"

His hand drifted to his leg but stopped short, clenching it into a fist instead. "Oh, doing well. No complaints."

"Good," she said. They stood in an awkward silence for a few moments. "Well, I need to be getting on with my day."

"Of course." His eyes drifted to the shotgun.

"The captain authorized it," Jasmine said.

Rollins nodded, then spoke in a low voice. "Keep your wits about you, eh? People are acting funny. Things going missing."

"Thanks," she said.

On the bridge, Jasmine sat at the map table and stared out the windows. An irritated Beaumont directed his ire at Chevket, who didn't seem to mind.

"The ballast, Mister Chevket, before we are all dead of old age."

"Sir."

Jasmine cleared her throat. "Will we be able to see the mountains soon?"

Beaumont let out a tight laugh. "Ryan willing, yes."

"And The Maw?"

Beaumont considered it for a moment. "Perhaps, yes. Ryan's arse, Mister Chevket, would you have us lost and circling in the desert? Correct two points to starboard."

"What is it, exactly?" she asked. Beaumont blew out his mustache and rose from his chair. Chevket, behind the captain, gave her a nod of thanks.

Beaumont walked to the map table and motioned her over. The map was spread out under glass with numbers and letters in grease pencil scrawled on top: windage, direction, and elevation.

"Attend: The Maw." He tapped a point marked with a strange spiral on the map. "Two maelstroms, one in the sea and its twin in the sky above. It is the airborne companion that draws the wind and shapes the clouds around us."

Jasmine stared at the map. "How big is it? How dangerous?"

"How dangerous is an enraged dragon? I saw it once when I was younger and more foolish. It inhaled clouds and churned them 'round until they were all like a shaggy ball in its gullet. Below, the waters swirled and bubbled, howling like a ravenous beast." He shook his head and grunted. "When they finished their meals, both spewed everything straight up into the atmosphere in a column so high, I couldn't see its end. The maelstroms never cease, only wax and wane. Fortunately, my foolhardy journey came during a waning phase. Any stronger and I would have found my little boat—and myself—consumed."

Jasmine followed their course marked in black grease pencil. "How close will we come?"

"Close enough to make landing a bit involved, but not so close as to make it difficult."

Beaumont stood and put a hand to his back. "Some traveling music, if you please, Mister Chevket."

Chevket looked up from a conversation with the helmsman. "Anything in particular, captain?"

"The usual," Beaumont said.

The bridge filled with steel guitar and twangy vocals. Jasmine bit her lip and took back all the bad things she had said about Bishop's power chords and Cally's bubblegum pop. Beaumont eased himself into his chair and tapped his foot in time. "Wonderful, isn't it? I find it perfect for these long journeys. No one understands our life like Blessed Willie Nelson, the Sanctified Nitty Gritty Dirt Band, and Alabama."

"I'm partial to Johnny Cash," Chevket murmured to Jasmine.

"I heard that," Beaumont said. "As I've always said, you may choose the music when you are captain of your own vessel, Chevket. There are not many perks to the position, but this is one of them."

A warbling "oo-oo-oo" echoed from the speaker and it was time to go.

The music blared throughout the ship, and to her horror, the crew enjoyed it. When they weren't eyeballing her as she passed, bodies tapped, hummed, and sang along to the steel guitars celebrating the simple life and all things redneck while also deriding anything urban or requiring more than two syllables of explanation. If only Ryan had lived through Nirvana, the music in this place might not be that bad. She could do with some Fiona Apple or Veruca Salt. If she ever discovered how to make it work, she'd introduce these people to her guilty pleasure, Celine Dion, too.

Yes, Jasmine, what this place needs is a few more divas.

She found refuge in the engine room with the necros and the deaders. The necros took their ease in worn denims and leather, lounging on chairs and smoking unfiltered cigarettes. Yolanda tipped an imaginary hat and blew a cloud of smoke towards the ceiling. Jasmine sat down on a nearby stool, back to the wall, with a clear view of the hatches.

"Nice shotgun. You look like crap," Yolanda said.

Acrid smoke ticked her nose. "Beaumont's choice in music and mine don't coincide."

"Willie Nelson, yeah?" Yolanda shrugged. "I didn't at first, but it got to grow on me. Can't play it in here though." At Jasmine's questioning look she waved the cigarette at the dynamos. "The deaders only know Badlands rock and roll. New-wave country from Paradise City interferes with their systems."

"Sure, why not?" Jasmine said. On the small stage, Corker stood over Snot-boy at the drum kit. Snot-boy had headphones covering one ear while Corker explained something to him in the other. Helgo plugged in a cord from the drum kit into one of the dynamo's coffins. "What's going on over there?" she asked.

Yolanda tossed her head. "Snot-boy's an apprentice so Corker's training him on direct-inject, feeding live music into the deaders instead of recorded tracks."

"Does that happen a lot?"

"Nah, it's a backup in case the tape deck goes down. Helgo claims you can eke out some extra efficiencies if you're a good enough necro, but I think he's full of shit."

"Why's that?"

"Watch."

Snot-boy's face took on an intense concentration as he gave a cymbal three experimental taps before erupting into motion. Without the soundtrack, it was all just a cacophony of thumping bass drum, crashing snare, and chaotic cymbals. Snot-boy seemed panicked, head darting left and right, arms flailing. Someone shouted, but he seemed oblivious. A red light flashed at the dynamo panel and Helgo threw a switch before rounding and charging the stage. A leather cowboy hat hit the youth in the face. Snot-boy jolted, all action coming to a sudden end. His face reddened, and he reached out to quiet a still-ringing cymbal.

"What is your major malfunction?" Helgo shouted. "You're rushing the down beat and your spazzing almost set off a neural cascade."

Snot-boy shrank on the stool. "Sorry."

Helgo took a deep breath. "Try it again. This time don't enter during a fill and keep it simple. I'll turn down the gain."

"That didn't go well, I take it," Jasmine said. Her eyes itched; she waved away the smoke.

Yolanda snorted. "It's like with the country music. The deaders only know the original recorded performances. Stray just a little, and their brains misfire. Then instead of happy deaders you have pissed-off deaders and pissed-off deaders throw off the whole load balance, which bollixes your dynamo, and bollixed dynamos go boom."

"Hence emergency only."

"Yeah, supposed to be." She dropped her cigarette and ground it out. "I gotta go walk the engine nacelles and make sure the deck apes haven't tripped over a power feed. Wanna come?"

"Does it involve narrow walkways and open sky?"

"Yes."

She shivered. "Then no."

"Suit yourself." She paused. "You came out of the Badlands, right?"

"I did."

"I've only heard stories second-hand. I'd love to hear about what you saw."

Jasmine's heart thumped louder and her stomach soured. She swallowed and shook her head. "You're busy. Maybe some other time."

Yolanda blinked. "Okay, sure. Whatever." She leaned in closer. "You know, some people in Paradise City will pay big money for Badlands relics. I'd be happy to look over any tools or kit you might have and arrange a meeting with a buyer once we get back."

Jasmine unclenched her hands and spread out her fingers on her lap. "The Caliphate captured me. They took everything."

"Oh." Yolanda looked away and brushed back a purple lock from her face. "Sorry, didn't mean to bring up bad memories." She glanced back. "If you ever want to talk…"

"Thanks." Jasmine gave a tight smile and let the silence stretch out until Yolanda hurried away.

~

JASMINE WATCHED the rest of the training session, Snot-boy eventually settling down into a more subdued performance meeting with Helgo's approval. He turned over the monitoring job to Dammit-Hammer and whistled at Jasmine's shotgun as he joined her.

"Got yourself the latest accessory."

"It just goes with every outfit I have," Jasmine said. "Who needs heels when you have a twelve-gauge?"

"You don't need that, you know. You're safe here."

Jasmine met his eyes. "No, I'm really not."

"Oh come on, that thing with the shield was a fluke. Bad timing"

She shook her head. "It's more than that." She checked to make sure the other necros were still occupied. "Someone broke into my room during the attack. Tossed it."

"Looking for what?"

"God knows. I don't know if I can sleep in there anymore."

"Did you tell the captain? You must have if he's letting you walk around armed."

"I told Chevket, or rather, he figured it out. He convinced the captain on my behalf. We're keeping it quiet until we can bring proof to Beaumont."

"Damn," Helgo said.

Jasmine looked down at her bracelet and gave it a twist. "I need your help, Helgo. I don't know who else to trust."

Helgo gave a short nod. "What do you need?"

"Whatever you can do. I was thinking you've been crawling all

85

through the ship all this time and the crew's used to that. You might be able to see or overhear something when their guard is down."

"Mind if I use the rest of the band? I won't give them any specifics."

Jasmine nodded. "Whatever you think best. Just be careful. For now whoever did it thinks they got away with it."

"All right. Hang on for a second." Helgo walked over to a tool chest and rummaged through several bins before coming back with a metal wedge.

"For your door. The bottom is rubber coated so it'll stay put."

He paused for a moment, then pulled something from a pocket and pressed it to her hand.

"I managed to scrounge this from the quartermaster. Serum, one dose. I still think it's a bad idea, but I promised."

Jasmine glanced at the small bag and cupped it under the door wedge. "Thanks, Helgo. I'll be careful."

JASMINE PAUSED at her door and made sure the passageway was clear. She strained on tiptoes and squinted in the dim light until she found the single hair stuck across the doorway with a bit of spittle—an old spy trick she had read about to tell if one's door had been opened. Inside, the *October's* slipstream whistled against the hull patches. Jasmine closed the door, kicking Helgo's wedge under it. She laid the shotgun on the bed and unrolled the small canvas bag containing a syringe and a vial of clear amber fluid. Her arm itched.

Well go ahead and do it, Jas, what are you waiting for?

No. She could hold out a bit longer. This was for emergencies only, if things got real bad. She rolled up the bag and poked about the room. After several minutes she figured out a way to stash the bag in the bed's hollow frame and undressed for the night, mindful of the shotgun at all times in case someone happened to burst through the door. She slipped under the sheets and leaned the shotgun against the wall within easy reach. The room was dark and quiet save for the whistling and the ship's distant groans and clanking.

She tried to sleep, but it was as if a presence lingered in the room, the faceless intruder in blood-soaked boots rummaging around, searching for her, turning to reveal the Caliph's bloated face leering, sausage-fingered hand dropping to his groin. He reached out—

Jasmine's eyes flew open, heart pounding and lungs struggling for air. Part of her was aware that she was alone in the room, but it did not have enough control to keep her from reaching out to the gun and snatching it as she scooted back and braced against the wall. Outside, footsteps approached and paused at her door. The shotgun barrel swung to the doorway. Her finger found the trigger and slid the safety off.

The shell is already in the chamber, no need to rack it.

The footsteps moved on, but Jasmine kept the gun trained on the door long after they departed, until her arms ached. She laid back and pulled the sheets up to her neck. The shotgun stayed beside her, tucked against her hip like a sleeping pet.

Nice job almost shooting blindly through the door, Goddess of Healing.

Shut up, me.

Oh poor mighty goddess!

"Shut up!" she said into the darkness

Her thoughts quieted for several minutes, and she began to drift.

What if the saboteur was being controlled like the Caliph? One of Ryan's avatars? They may not even remember what they did.

Her eyes flew open. "Fuck," she whispered and flung the covers away. She returned to bed with the bottle.

Weak. You're so weak.

Jasmine shrugged and took a swig. At least it was the lesser of two evils.

12

———

Jasmine woke without knowing why. Her heart raced and she had the sense of something loud in her ears. There was a shadow under the door—two feet shuffling. She reached for the shotgun and trained it on the door, thumbing the safety off. It was risky, sleeping with a shell in the chamber, but there would be no *click-clack* warning as she racked in a shell, just a boom.

A soft knock sounded, a finger tapping. "Miss Shaw? Miss Shaw? It's Chevket. I need to speak with you."

She sat in the dark and took in several deep breaths until her heart settled down.

"Just a moment," she called out and turned on a lamp, wincing and blinking away purple after-images. She gave her blankets a snap, sending the remnants of tonight's snack (yesterday's bread) flying. She sat up, fully dressed but for her shoes, having decided she couldn't afford the vulnerability of the nightgown Chevket had somehow found for her. She slid into her shoes and wiggled her heels until they fit.

"Miss Shaw?"

"In a minute." She slid the wedge out from under the door and retreated to the bed, shotgun at the ready. She gave her bracelet a twist.

"Enter."

The door cracked open and Chevket's curly-haired head poked in. His mouth pursed at the shotgun not quite pointed in his direction but didn't say anything. The rest of his lanky body entered, and he closed the door quietly behind him.

"Is that really necessary?"

Jasmine gave a small shrug. "Maybe not, but why chance it?"

Chevket nodded and looked around the room. He pointed at the heavy wedge. "Perhaps I could replace this under the door. Would that make you feel... secure?"

Jesus, he thinks I'm a rabid dog or something.

Maybe you are.

Shut up.

She forced a smile. "Sure. That works." She put the shotgun aside, though not until after Chevket set the wedge in place.

"What is it?" she asked.

"I was thinking about the incident in your room and wonder if the culprit wasn't searching for an artifact of some sort from the Badlands."

"You're the second person to ask me about that."

"Really? Who?"

"Yolanda down in the engine room wanted to know about the Badlands, the Caliphate and all that, but I didn't want to talk about it. Then she wanted to look at anything a collector in Paradise City might want."

He slouched against the door and rubbed at his eyes. "I understand. And while you may not want to talk about it, I must press you on this. The Badlands, for all its problems, is powerfully tied to the Creator. Many recovered weapons and holy relics have powers not seen elsewhere."

"The Caliph's men captured us outside the Badlands and took it all. We lost the crossbow and the shotgun, and we certainly didn't have any holy relics. I don't even recall seeing a church."

"Nothing at all, not even jewelry or trinkets?"

She paused, and her eyes dropped to the bracelet she was absently twisting on her wrist.

"Just this bracelet. I made it from Cally's ribbon and Bishop's guitar strings."

Chevket sucked in a breath through his teeth. "Brother Bishop, the Landweaver?"

"I only knew him as Bishop, but there was a statue of him in the city with that name."

"May I see them for a moment?"

Jasmine paused then chided herself for being irrational. The strings chafed as she slid them off and exposed angry red marks crisscrossing her wrist. She felt oddly exposed and clamped her hand over the raw skin.

Chevket turned the bracelet over in his hands and scraped a fingernail across the strings' ridges.

"Well?"

His thumb rubbed across Cally's yellow ribbon. "I'm surprised no one could feel their power, but perhaps you have to be holding them to notice, or maybe your own power drowns them out. Could you imagine a guitar strung with the Landweaver's strings?" He let out a low whistle.

"Does everyone have two names around here?"

He smiled. "Just the important people. I imagine you have one already."

Jasmine squirmed and glanced away. "I don't know if I want to know."

"I would guess 'Jasmine the Redeemer,'" Chevket said softly. His fingernail picked at the ribbon's thick knot.

Phantom ants crawled down her spine. "Stop that."

"Sorry. I never thought I would hold an artifact of power. That only happens to important people."

"You're holding one now. Maybe this means someday you will have two names."

His eyes brightened, and he grinned. "Wouldn't that be something?" He handed the bracelet back to her. "I would recommend you put it in the captain's safe, but I doubt you'd listen to me?"

She nodded.

"Then please keep it on you at all times, but hidden. It's probably worth more than ten *October Skys*."

～

In the morning, Jasmine took breakfast with the captain in his quarters.

"What bothers me, Miss Shaw, is that the raid happened at all. Bad enough luck to stumble across a squadron on patrol rather than a single scout, worse still to have them come upon us at the very moment our shields were inoperable." Beaumont rocked forward on his elbows. "It was my responsibility and my mistake to allow Mister Helgo his little upgrade, and for my part, I could have doomed the mission."

Jasmine wanted to comfort the captain but didn't know how. However, he had given her an opening.

"Unless..." She swirled a spoon through her coffee, not meeting his gaze.

"Unless what, Miss Shaw?"

"Unless someone's been feeding the Caliphate our position and moments of weakness."

Beaumont's face went hard, and he leaned back. "That is possible," he said with a tight nod. "I should wonder who on board would do such a thing. This is hardly the first time we've tangled with the Caliphate. Why betray us now?"

"You're familiar with the phrase 'Badlands born, Badlands cursed?'"

"Superstitious poppycock."

"Maybe not." She let out a ragged breath. "I have powers others don't. A single drop of my blood can heal mortal wounds. I brought dead trees back to life, cured diseases, neutralized poisons. Doesn't my curse have to balance that out?"

"I have heard stories like this before. I have also, more than any other in the fleet, flown missions in the Badlands and many so-called powers are much exaggerated or non-existent altogether. I admit many possess remarkable talents and aptitudes, but nothing years of careful practice or cultivation cannot match or exceed. Outside of your brother the Creator, that is, and his long-dead disciples.

"I also admit you may in fact have power, perhaps fantastic power. My point is that even with all I have seen, I've found no evidence of this fabled curse, only misfortunes and bad luck. In your own case, I believe our pursuers are after us for your political value more than any other consideration. There is no supernatural curse at work, merely ugly human nature."

Jasmine sipped at her coffee. "Even if it is only that, is it not enough for someone to sell us out?"

Beaumont frowned as she drank. Finally, he sniffed and rubbed at his forehead.

"It may, though the level of coordination and access is damned troubling."

"Who would be able to do this?"

Beaumont thought for a moment. "Anyone with relatively unrestricted access to the ship, the ability to communicate with the Caliphate, and inner knowledge of the maintenance plans. Unfortunately, that describes many: the senior crew, the marines, and the necros."

"How does this change the mission?" Jasmine asked.

"It doesn't. It means we stay vigilant, tighten security. Perhaps search the *October Sky* from top to bottom and see what shakes loose."

"Won't that tip off our saboteur?"

"Perhaps it will, and he will go to ground. Either we catch him outright, or else he lies low for a while, which will give us more time to reach our destination."

13

———————

She found the body by accident. She had been walking through the *October Sky's* envelope, its bouquets of individual air cells creating a bulbous forest. Technically she should have been escorted by Chevket or Helgo, but they were busy and she couldn't stand sitting around. A scent of burning metal and barbecue led her around until she found strands of purple hair sticking out from under a conduit. She put the shotgun to her shoulder and approached, her heart sounding a drumbeat in her ears.

Yolanda's eyes stared at nothing, a surprised look on her face. An arm holding wire cutters bent in too many places and the boot on her left foot had no heel, only charred flesh. Partially melted wires hung from a blackened junction box above her.

Are we so used to dead bodies, now?

Shut up, me.

"What were you doing, Yo?" Jasmine said as much to block out her thoughts as anything else. The necro surely knew enough not to cut live wires, hadn't she? Jasmine scanned the deck. She found Yo's toolbox farther down the way, arcane implements arranged like a puzzle so as to take up the least amount of space. A slip of paper sat under the toolbox. Jasmine knelt and read it, a series of numbers that tugged at her memory, but she couldn't place them.

"Miss Shaw?"

Jasmine pivoted, bringing the shotgun to bear on Chevket and two marines with hands on their sidearms. The man remained unperturbed even as his marines flinched.

"I didn't do it," she blurted.

Way to look guilty, Jas.

Chevket pursed his lips. "The *October Sky* just lost its port engine array and now it would appear that there has been an accident." He turned to one of the marines. "Inform the captain and request he come here." To the other he said, "Secure the area and make sure no one approaches until the captain arrives."

Jasmine lowered the shotgun and went over to the first officer. He looked at Yo's body dispassionately, eyes flicking from the body to the cutters in her hand and then to the junction box. "The captain ordered the engines powered down until we determine the problem and fix it, I am... I don't know." He ran a hand through his curls.

"There's more over here," Jasmine said, and led him to the toolbox and note.

"Heading, speed, and an ETA on our destination," Chevket said with a single look. "The first two she read in the engine bay or the bridge, the last a trivial calculation if one knows our destination."

An ice ball settled in Jasmine's stomach. "Yolanda was our spy?" She shook her head. "Something's not right."

Chevket slowly nodded. "Perhaps she was part of a team."

"Maybe."

"You suspect otherwise?"

Jasmine pointed from Yolanda's corpse to her toolbox. "If she were working here, why leave all her tools over there? It would be real inconvenient if you needed something. Plus, she's no dummy. I don't see her accidentally cutting into a power cable."

"It is dark, and she may have been in a hurry. Even the best of us are careless in such situations."

Jasmine crouched down and closed Yolanda's eyelids. "Yes, that's true I suppose." Jasmine thought back to her room after the attack. "There's panic here, a carelessness that means either our enemy is desperate, or they just don't think we'll figure it out before it's too late."

Footsteps banged across the deck and a red-faced Beaumont rounded the corner.

"Blast it to the maelstroms, Chevket! What happened here?"

Chevket gave his little nod-bow. "Sabotage."

"Damn necros, and only a day's flight away from Utopia." Beaumont muttered.

Jasmine's fist tightened around the shotgun's sling. Chevket quickly spoke. "Perhaps not, sir. Miss Shaw thinks this a clumsy ruse."

"Ruse? A ruse for what?"

"What if she came across the real saboteur, and this is just an improvised way to throw us off?" Jasmine said.

Beaumont glowered. "What if, what if, what if! Meanwhile, our pursuit comes ever closer while we have only the choice of drifting with the wind or turning lazy circles with one blasted set of engines."

Chevket waved a hand at the mess of wires. "For all the damage, I can have it repaired within the hour."

"See to it, Chevket." Beaumont strode over to a panel and blew into the speaking tube. "Bridge, this is the captain. Raise shields, alert status Bravo. Repeat: raise shields, alert status Bravo." He held the tube to his ear and grunted as a voice confirmed.

Jasmine said, "We're running out of time."

Beaumont shook his head. "We will complete this mission, Miss Shaw. There is simply no other alternative. Chevket! Sweep the critical systems in teams of two or more for any other signs of sabotage."

Chevket's eyes momentarily narrowed before he regained his composure and simply replied "Sir."

"You're very demanding of him, captain," Jasmine said.

Beaumont drew himself up and placed his hands behind his back. "Miss Shaw, when one is in command, one does not say please. Kindly return to your quarters until I send Chevket to fetch you."

"I'm not under your command, captain."

Beaumont's jaw clicked. "Allow me to do my job, on my ship, madam. Your wandering about with a potential saboteur loose makes it that much more difficult."

Jasmine folded her arms.

Beaumont spoke through clenched teeth. "Please."

Jasmine nodded. "I'll be in my quarters, waiting for Mister Chevket."

~

Jasmine set her food reserves on the bed and decided it was time to replace the brown-skinned fruit with something more durable. She absently pulled at the wine bottle.

Empty.

Her eyes settled on the bed's far corner and the deader serum in its little canvas pouch. Maybe just a half dose? No. She could hold out until dinner tonight and sneak another wine bottle when Beaumont was distracted. She placed the serum at the bottom of a knapsack made from her pillowcase and wire from Helgo's supply reels. After the serum came the food and extra shotgun shells. Everything she possessed fit with room left over.

She wished she could find some oil for the shotgun and maybe someone to teach her how to clean and care for it. She knew it needed to be oiled, was it supposed to be done periodically, or after firing it, or both? She wished she had her crossbow; she understood how that worked, but as she racked out the shells and fed them back in to the shotgun she realized how little she knew. Point the barrel, pull the trigger, and pump in a new shell. More moving parts, more chances of failure.

The klaxons blared, and Jasmine jumped, smacking her elbow against the wall. She tossed the knapsack in her footlocker, slung the shotgun over her shoulder, and ran out the door, her feet crashing on the deck and eyes scanning the passing faces for any signs that one might reach out and grab her in the chaos.

The bridge was steeped in the same tension as their escape from Paradise City. Beaumont, buckled in his command chair, glanced at her as she strapped into an empty chair at the map table.

"It seems the Caliph's forces have caught us adrift. Rather convenient, wouldn't you say? And with a favorable mix of 'thopters and gunboats supporting a zeppelin raider, doubtlessly filled with the requisite number of foolhardy pirates with which to board and capture us as prize."

Jasmine nodded. "What are our options?"

Beaumont blew out his mustache and drummed his fingers. "Run or fight, where neither option holds promise. Until we get those engines operable, we fight as best we can, and pick off those that cannot hold formation. With luck, we can keep their boarding craft at bay."

He swung back and dictated orders. Jasmine checked the mirrors. Tiny motes that must have been the 'thopters swirled around larger, fatter shapes like bumblebees or obese dragonflies—the gunboats. Behind them, the dusty orange lozenge of the raiding zeppelin, of similar size to the *October Sky* though not as well maintained, its envelope patched and lumpy.

"Fire pattern Theta," Beaumont said.

The electro-guns fired, sending fuzzy balls of glowing plasma into the gunboat formations. The enemy broke, the 'thopters easily avoiding the danger while the larger craft lagged a few seconds behind. The raiders regrouped and approached, cannon shells from the gunboats bracketing the *October Sky*.

"They're focusing on the engine pods," someone called out.

"Load aft cannon with flack. Electros, bracket those gunboats."

As the salvos fired, a pattern emerged. The incoming gunboats and their ornithopter escorts were forced into an area where the *October Sky's* tail gunners could easily pick them off or force them into black shrapnel-filled clouds. The raiders' alternative was peeling away from the *October Sky* altogether and taking a long looping path back. The shields sparked and flared but withstood the incoming fire.

Chevket entered the bridge and took up his station.

"Any other signs of sabotage?" Beaumont said.

"Nothing obvious, captain," he said. The speaking tube whistled, and Chevket leaned down to listen. "Mister Helgo reports the engine damage repaired."

"Helm?" Beaumont said.

"Engines responding."

"Very well. Ahead full and keep that carrier from stealing our wind. Blessed Saint Willy, may the ammunition hold out."

"Contact ahead!"

Chevket startled. "What?" He ran over and grabbed the officer's binoculars.

"Report!" Beaumont said.

Chevket swallowed. "Sir. Confirm four pursuit ships, ours."

"Do you recognize them?"

"They look like the First Pursuit Squadron."

A glowing object dropped from each ship, and they broke formation. "They're burning through deaders like candy to catch us," Beaumont muttered. "How inefficient. Very well. Helm, put us on an intercept course with the pursuit boats and get me a signalman. Chevket!"

The first offer shook himself and his face flushed. "Sir?"

"To your station, man. We're going to lay ourselves on the anvil and try to jump before the hammer strikes. Inform the engine room to prepare sonic countermeasures."

The floor beneath Jasmine began vibrating, like a wasp's nest had built itself into her chair. Jasmine's eyes met Chevket's, now flat and unemotional. "Sonic incursion. The necros on the pursuit boats are trying disrupt our power systems."

"You mean the deaders."

"As you say." Little nod. "They will try inducing noise or disruptive harmonics on our shields to back-feed into the power cells. Mister Helgo will thwart them by modulating our shields and programming the appropriate sonics for our deaders."

"What happens if they succeed?"

"Power surges, disrupted energy flows, in rare cases the whole dynamo blows its stack. Excuse me," Chevket said and leaned into the speaker tube to listen to a report.

The cannonade behind them increased in intensity as the Caliphate forces grew closer. Beaumont murmured in the signalman's ear, and the man began clacking the message at the approaching squadron on his signal lantern. The Caliphate swarm darted around the flack and came at the *October Sky* from different angles. The ornithopters swooped ahead of the gunboats, firing their machine guns into the *October's* shields trying to bring them down with sheer brute force. The Paradise City squadron split into pairs, signal lights twinkling from the lead boat.

"May Ricky Skaggs curse them to hell!" Beaumont said. "'Heave to and prepare to be boarded' indeed! Pursuit captains must be chosen for pure arrogance over actual intelligence. Helm, come about to 270.

Gunnery, rig cannon for point defense, electros prepare focus fire on the *Kashmir* if fired upon."

"*Kashmir* and *Immigrant Song* on intercept, captain," Chevket said. "The *Black Dog* and *Misty Mountain* appear to be maneuvering to engage the carrier."

"Fools that they are," Beaumont murmured. He glanced at the mirrors and let out a laugh. "But thank Blessed Ryan for fools! We may get out of this yet."

"Did my brother happen to name those ships?" Jasmine asked Chevket.

"I believe he did, miss."

"Of course he did," she said, shaking her head.

Nearly all the ornithopters peeled away from the *October Sky* to meet the *Immigrant Song* while the *Black Dog* and *Misty Mountain* began exchanging salvos with the carrier. In the confusion, one of the *October's* electro-guns spat a globe of plasma into a Caliphate gunboat which exploded and rained shrapnel on the *October's* shields. A cheer rose up only to be cut short by exploding debris opening a hole in the shields. Another gunboat changed course and dove for the breach.

"Up thirty on the elevators. Rapid fire the aft turrets," Beaumont said.

With agonizing slowness, the hole began closing. Heavy fire raked the gunboat, which shuddered with near misses but kept coming. As it neared the breach, a plasma globe hit it from above. The craft slewed away, trailing smoke.

"*Immigrant Song*, sir," Chevket said.

Beaumont grunted. "They may be arrogant, but their gunnery is first-rate."

Then the whole ship groaned around them, and Jasmine's teeth rattled. The wail of guitars and driving bass buzzed through the floor, a half beat out of synch with the *October's* usual vibrations.

"They've found a resonance!" Chevket shouted. Outside, the shields flared then winked out.

"Sound the dive alarm. Emergency vent to 500 meters. The bastards save us only to kill us themselves," Beaumont said. A shrill klaxon sounded.

"Hang on tight, Miss Shaw," Chevket said. No sooner had the words left his mouth when the floor dropped out from under her. The battle around the *October Sky* soared away, and Jasmine clutched at the seatbelt around her waist. Her stomach convulsed so she closed her eyes, telling herself not to throw up. At least the off-beat music had stopped. She took in quick breaths, and the nausea subsided. The *October Sky's* fall tapered off though the windows filled with closer ground views than seemed safe.

Beaumont turned about as he issued orders. "Topside batteries prioritize gunboats. Helm, come about to 290. Level the elevators. Damage report."

Above them, the *Kashmir* and *Immigrant Song* traded fire with the remaining gunboat.

Chevket straightened from the speaking tube. "Power surge in the engine room, Helgo reports the dynamo is damaged but still functional."

"Tell him to get those shields back, Chevket."

"Sir."

Something flashed, and Jasmine glanced up. The last Caliphate gunboat had pulled away from the pursuit boats, heading at them with a single ornithopter flying before it. The 'thopter grew, dagger-like and blood red, corkscrewing around the topside battery fire and closing fast.

Beaumont saw it too.

"It's going to punch straight through the envelope. Roll twenty degrees and fire all batteries. Bring that kamikaze down!"

Jasmine was thrown to the side as the *October Sky* rolled on its long axis and the air between the ornithopter and the airship filled with bullets, flack, and plasma. The 'thopter jinked and rolled in ways that should have turned its pilot into jelly and yet it came on, nimbly picking its way through the deadly blossoms. Jasmine could almost make out the pilot through his windscreen.

So this is how it ends. You know what Cally would do.

She lifted an arm and raised her middle finger.

The pilot wore no helmet. Wild black hair framed a scowling face streaked with blood flowing from his eyes, staring right at her.

Kikuchiyo. The Blood Weeper.

Oh shit.

The Blood Weeper's 'thopter grew impossibly large as time slowed. Just before it struck the *October's* envelope, Kikuchiyo leapt from the cockpit. The *October Sky* shook with a thunderclap and more alarms blared around her along with calls for reserve helium. The Blood Weeper's body lay limp on a spar jutting from the envelope's top. There was no way a body could have survived the impact, but Jasmine kept watching as the crew scrambled around her.

"Gunboat incoming. Prepare to repel boarders!"

Did a finger just twitch?

"The 'thopter took out the dorsal turret!"

"Shields back up."

A finger definitely moved.

"Venting arrested, but reserves empty."

Kikuchiyo's head rolled, and a bloody eyelid opened.

"Captain," Jasmine said.

"Caliphate 'thopters destroyed. *Kashmir's* disengaged and trailing smoke, *Immigrant Song* closing."

"Captain," Jasmine said louder.

"What about the *Black Dog* and *Misty Mountain*? The carrier?"

"No eyes on them, captain."

"Very well."

The Blood Weeper's hand closed in a fist.

"Miss Shaw?" Chevket said.

Jasmine pointed. The Weeper's fist trembled.

"Captain!" Jasmine fumbled at her seatbelt.

"Blast it, madam, what—" He saw their faces and looked to the mirror.

"Bugger," Beaumont said. "Right. Mister Chevket, open the weapons locker and then escort Miss Shaw to a launch. Fly her to the objective while we cover your escape."

"Sir." He pulled a key from his belt and went to a weapons locker.

"I'm not running away," Jasmine said, ignoring the voice in her head clamoring for just that.

"I agree," Beaumont said. "You are continuing on with your mission, Miss Shaw, and doing your duty as I will do mine."

"No, I'm not letting you sacrifice yourselves for me."

"Miss Shaw, it is not up to you whether I or this ship obeys your wishes at this point. The battle is joined." He waved at the ships firing on each other around them "Besides, so long as my antagonists continue behaving foolishly by splitting their forces, the *October Sky* will slip through and catch you up. But not if you keep yammering at me."

"But the Blood Weeper—"

"Am I not the captain of this ship? Not your concern! Now go!"

Chevket put a hand on her shoulder and pulled her towards the hatchway. She shook it off and gave him a glare. "Don't do that again." She turned to Beaumont and summoned up a mighty lie. "I've dealt with the Blood Weeper before. Leave him to me. Your duty right now is keeping the *October Sky* in one piece."

Beaumont grimaced and reluctantly nodded. "Take Chevket with you then and good luck."

Beaumont turned back to the battle. "Focus the sonics on *Immigrant Song* and give 'em a dose of the Man in Black."

Chevket touched her arm and snatched it back at her glare. "Miss Shaw?"

"Let's go topside."

14

———

Jasmine's feet pounded the deck, skittering to a halt as she caught the first ladder to the upper deck.

"Jasmine! Not that way," Chevket called out.

"This is the quickest way."

"It's right where the gunboat is cutting through. We'll go around." He ran past, waving her along.

She ground her teeth. "We don't have the time!"

Chevket sprinted through the passageways without looking back. Exploding shells rattled windows, and Jas blinked away purple afterimages as blue-white electros splattered across the shield. Her legs burned as she barely kept Chevket's slim form in sight. She passed another topside ladder and wondered how many more they would bypass. She had crawled through every area of the ship, and they were almost at the *October Sky's* aft end. Was her mental map wrong? Surely they had cleared the gunboat.

She turned a corner and shouted at Chevket clambering down a ladder.

"That's the launch bay!"

"Access ladder 11A," he called back.

Her stomach clenched as her mental map caught up. 11A led to the ship's rudder–outside. "I don't do heights!"

"The forward access hatch is too close to the gunboat. Probably their primary target. This is all we've got."

She dropped the last foot into the launch bay, a tight space with two 'thopters hanging in their cradles above bomb bay-style doors. Past them an oblong hatch led to a simple ladder and naked sky. Chevket stood to the side, playing out a short length of rope with a carabiner at each end.

"Chevket, I can't."

"You won't fall, Jasmine. You clip one end to your belt, the other to the handrail."

He opened the door. Smoke trailed behind the *October Sky*. A few remaining enemy 'thopters ran the flack gauntlet and strafed the shields, pulling away before getting caught in the crossfire between *October Sky* and *Kashmir*. From some trick of the shield or wind, rifle fire and shouting marines repelling boarders reached her ears.

"They've already breached," Chevket said. He ducked under a 'thopter's open gull-wing door and held up the safety rope. "Quickly. I'll hook you in."

Jasmine swallowed. The dunes rolled beneath them, and the *October's* slipstream battered her face. Her throat seized, and the room started spinning. She closed her eyes and locked her knees, placing a hand against the 'thopter door for support.

"I can't do it."

"You won't have to."

She opened her eyes to Chevket's vicious smile. He lunged. They tumbled into the 'thopter. She scrambled on hands and knees away from him, fumbling at the shotgun. His hand caught her ankle, and she kicked out, clipping him on the jaw. The gun slapped into her hands, and she twisted, leveling the barrel inches from Chevket's forehead.

Do it.

She pulled the trigger.

Click.

The safety was off.

Chevket grinned through his split lip, perfect white teeth outlined in blood. She pumped the action, sending the unfired shell to the deck and racking another in.

Click.

She pumped in a new shell.

Click.

Chevket smirked. "Hard to blow my head off without a firing pin, isn't it, Jasmine?"

She swung the shotgun around, but he caught it mid-swing and forced it between them before falling on her with his whole weight. The shotgun lay across her chest between them, crushing her ribcage. Chevket did a little push-up, and it was all she could do to keep breathing.

"Kikuchiyo is all rage and anger," he said. "He's never had vision, no aspirations beyond removing heads from bodies. He'd kill you and it would be a waste, Jasmine, when you are worth so much more alive."

"Traitor," Jasmine gasped. Chevket shoved and forced the air from her lungs.

"I'm not built from depraved lust like the old Caliph, or anger like the Blood Weeper. You'll find me more than fair and rewarding but don't doubt I'll get what I want one way or another." He brought his face to hers, and she could pick out every clogged pore in his nose, smell the spiced tea and sour milk on his breath. "When I'm running the new Caliphate, I promise you'll be treated well. Or you and your two names can die here." Jasmine's vision went black at the edges. "Join me."

His body shifted on hers, and she managed a half gasp and before the crushing weight could return, she snapped her head forward. She saw pink stars as her skull crashed into Chevket's. She didn't give him time to react, bringing her head back and snapping forward again. Something crunched and crumbled beneath her forehead. She repeated the head butt one last time as her vision had narrowed to a pinprick. His weight vanished, and she took in the sweetest breath of her life. Chevket's grip loosened on the barrel while his other hand went to his nose, now gushing blood like a faucet.

They roared at the same time, Chevket's forearm leveled at her throat, Jasmine swinging the shotgun's stock at his temple. The walnut stock hit him squarely and sent his head wobbling. Chevket's blow slammed into her collar bone, snapping it with a sensation like a miniature sun exploding. She rolled away, screaming as the broken ends ground against each other.

Chevket moaned and breathed wetly.

She pulled herself up using her good arm. Chevket had a bloody mess where his nose used to be and a dent in his skull, which probably explained why his eyes weren't focusing. She hadn't even stopped to ask what Cally would have done, but she suspected her friend would have approved.

Speaking of Cally.

I know.

She gripped the shotgun like a staff and brought it down on Chevket's head, over and over again until he stopped moving. She felt like collapsing but instead staggered from the 'thopter and grabbed a safety line. She thought about going back and grabbing Chevket's pistol, but when it came to the Blood Weeper, guns were useless. She stepped through the oblong hatch and made her way up the ladder, too tired or too crazy to worry about the height.

JASMINE WAS grateful for the broken collar bone. The pain focused her on the mechanics of climbing and not the open air beneath or the battle going on around her. She pinned her right arm against herself and concentrated: left arm up, step, step, repeat. The safety line's carabiner pulled and scratched at the metal cable running alongside the ladder like taking a reluctant dog for a walk. Something exploded overhead and the ladder shook; a hot knife twisted in her shoulder. She screwed her eyes shut and rode through it with quick, shallow breaths. The pain ebbed, and she reached for the next rung. While cuts healed quickly, resetting bones evidently took longer.

Or the break is worse than you thought. Maybe if someone set it straight. Maybe if we focused on healing ourselves instead of others, Jas.

No time. Never enough time.

At the ladder's top, the *October's* rudder loomed taller than a house. She knelt and made a quick switch from the ladder's safety cable to another strung across the envelope. Only the *Immigrant Song* remained nearby, trading salvos with the *October Sky*. The air between them shimmered with electro bolts and flaring shield hits; cannon fire poured

106

through the breaches, leaving blackened holes large and small across each envelope. Unless she missed her mark, each ship was blasting weaponized country music and 70s stoner rock at the other. High above, the Caliphate carrier spewed flames and the *Black Dog* and *Misty Mountain* retreated, heavily damaged themselves. To her left, the Caliphate gunboat hung from the *October Sky* like a giant swollen tick. She headed for the dorsal turret's remains, pushing the pace as fast as her shoulder would allow, barely above a walk. As she came on the turret, she swallowed.

The Blood Weeper pushed to one knee, blood dripping from his face onto the *October's* smooth skin. She didn't know what she was going to do. No plan. What the fuck was she thinking?

He turned and stood with a scowl but made no move toward her. Just like the bastard, to make her walk the whole way. Jasmine took a step and was pulled up short, sending another knife twisting into her shoulder. She hissed and found her safety cable snagged in the turret's wreckage. She unclipped her line and took a wobbly step.

Don't fall don't fall don't fall.

The Blood Weeper's hand went to the paired swords at his waist, settling on the longer, the *katana*. She took a step forward with legs fighting the vibrations beneath her feet. The Blood Weeper, still holding himself awkwardly as his bones shifted and re-knitted under his skin, remained perfectly balanced on the balls of his feet, watching her as she took another wobbly step. Her body felt numb, she couldn't breathe, but she kept putting one foot in front of the other, ignoring the part of her screaming to run away.

She stopped a few paces away. The Weeper just watched, oblivious to the battle still raging around them. A bone in his face set with a wet crunch and he grunted.

The muscles in her own shoulder twisted and cramped. She cried out and went to one knee as the collar bone realigned, then fused with a snap and flash of pain almost as bad as the original break. The cramp loosened and left her hyperventilating for several seconds before she got it under control and managed to stand. Her shoulder was sore and weak, but it worked.

Just in time to die.

Shut up, me.

"Well, Kikuchiyo?" she said. "Here I am. Leave the rest of the crew alone."

He shouted at her in Japanese.

"English, please."

The Blood Weeper's knee aligned with a wet crunch. He winced, then lowered himself into a crouch and angled his shoulder, thumbing the *katana* an inch from its sheath. He shuffled a half-step closer.

"Were you in with Chevket?"

The Blood Weeper gave a grunt almost in disappointment and leapt, twisting in the air, *katana* unsheathed. The sword flashed with the reflected blue-white actinic flare of electro-gun fire, and she picked out the wavy line where the sword's spine gave way to its edge, almost on her now. She closed her eyes despite herself.

Sorry, Bishop, I fucked up.

A breeze whispered across her face, and a thump sounded to her left. She opened her eyes to find Kikuchiyo crouched beside her, sword extended before him with blood on its tip.

"You didn't flinch," he said. He stood and gave her a nod. "Chevket." He spat at her feet.

"He didn't think much of you either. He's dead now. Was he like you, like the Caliph, one of Ryan's avatars?"

Kikuchiyo grunted. "Ambition without honor."

"Like how you ran Bishop off a cliff? Like how you stabbed Cally through the back? What honor do you have?"

Fresh blood flowed from his eyes. "No honor."

Something tickled under her left eye, now beginning to burn. Jasmine reached up and came away with red fingertips. Her eyes went from her bloody fingertips to the Weeper's red-streaked face. An idea formed, and she pressed her hand to her wound, blood seeping between her fingers. He cocked the sword's hilt to his ear in a two-handed grip.

"Die well."

"We are the same, Kikuchiyo," she said.

"Not the same."

She closed her fist. "Wanna bet?" She swung and flicked her fingers at him. He turned but not before the splatter hit his face. His head snapped back as if she had punched him. Then his features melted and began re-arranging themselves.

He sank to his knees, and began slipping down the envelope. She grabbed at his kimono's lapel and held him up until his face disappeared and her brother stared back at her. He cried out, head snapping around at the plasma and explosions blooming around them.

"Ryan," she said.

"This isn't real," he said. Then he looked at her. "I'm dreaming again," he said with a small laugh.

On the Caliph's ship, in the tiny hell known as the *hareem,* Jasmine had almost lost her mind, keeping only a tiny flame alive in the deepest part of her psyche. She had forgotten that flame as she had tried forget-ting about what happened in the Caliph's bedroom, her blood trans-forming the Caliph and forcing Ryan to the surface. The flame in her mind erupted and she remembered everything.

She laid a hand on Ryan's face. "Can you feel that?"

"Yes."

She punched him twice. "Then you're not dreaming!" She punched him again. Again. Her foot caught his ribs and left him gasping. His body slid down, and she lunged for him, pulling him back up to his wobbly feet. She shoved with one hand and grabbed the kimono's sash with the other. His arms windmilled and dropped the *katana.*

"Wait!" Ryan said. "I'm sorry, it wasn't my fault."

She drew her fist back.

"I mean it was, but it wasn't," he said quickly. "Listen, I can fix this. I am fixing this."

"People are dying because of you, Ryan. Bishop is dead. Cally is dead. More are dying right now."

"It's not as simple as waving my hand, all right? Change one thing, and four others turn to shit. It's not like I don't care! Look, I'm the good guy here."

Jasmine shook him. "You are the Blood Weeper, and you are trying to kill me. You were Chevket and tried kidnapping me. You were the Caliph and you..." The words froze in her throat and her brain refused to look. She swallowed. "How many others? You're not fixing it, Ryan, you're just making it worse."

"I can't control them, not yet. But you can help me," he said. "Please, I am so sorry for everything. I will make this right between us and can make it all work. Don't you understand? I'm a *god* here. You can be a god too. These people you're worried about it's not like they're real, Jasmine. We can always make—" and he screamed as Jasmine let the sash slip and he tottered.

Jasmine shook her head. "You're not a god. You're a fuck-up who died in a bloody heap on the side of the road."

He blinked. The fear drained from him, and he scowled. "Okay. I see how it is now. I could have let you slip into the void when you died, little miss perfect, but I saved you. 'Thanks a lot, brother of mine?' No, just bitching about things you don't understand."

"I understand enough," Jasmine said.

"Think so?" The skin on his face drooped, an eyelid spasmed. "I feel your power fading."

She wiped more blood on his face, and he laughed. "It doesn't work that way. I know the way back to my body now, so go ahead and let go. I'll be fine."

"I'm coming for you."

The skin flowed across his eyes and nose, a store mannikin's face. "Come find me, Jas, and don't die on the way. And if you don't want more dead friends, come alone."

A moment later, Kikuchiyo's face returned. The samurai's eyes went wide with panic.

"Your god left you," Jasmine said shifting her grip. "I have only one question: can you fly?"

His hand flew to the *katana's* scabbard but grasped only air. He reached for his other sword too late. Jasmine held it, scabbard and all, before her as he slid away. The Blood Weeper howled as he bounced once against the *October Sky's* envelope before dropping through the shield. She tucked the sword into her belt and walked to the nearest hatch.

15

Kikuchiyo's short sword, while not a gun, gave her confidence. The blade ran just longer than her forearm, deadly sharp and light as air. It vibrated in her hand like an eager dog on a leash, ready to lop off fingers and limbs. Gunfire from the bridge echoed in the passageways, so Jasmine ran for the engine room, making a quick stop on the way to grab her knapsack.

She caught the scent of barbecue and steeled her stomach before she came upon the bodies neatly stacked in a macabre pyramid outside the engine room's hatch. The luckless raiders had a bloated look with dark splotches around the hands and feet. They hadn't been cooked with fire, maybe electricity?

She looked past the bodies to the metal hatch and the dog-wheel mounted to the right. She grabbed a broom from a nearby locker and banged on the hatch.

"Helgo, it's me!"

The intercom next to the door squawked. "What was the name of the song I used on the overseer?"

Jasmine pressed the button. "I don't fucking remember, Helgo!"

"Then bugger off, I'm busy."

She jammed the button. "I'm no good with 80s music trivia. You owe me, Helgo, remember?"

"Okay, just sing a little bit of it then."

She grimaced. "It was something like 'bop-bwaa-da, bop-bwaa-da...'"

"Close enough, hang on."

The dog-wheel turned and Helgo met her with a black-toothed grin.

"The correct answer was 'Goody Two Shoes' by Adam Ant."

"Just let me in," she said, checking to make sure more Caliphate raiders weren't rounding the corner.

Helgo stepped aside and dogged the door shut as she pushed through.

"Securing the hatch!" he shouted, receiving several 'rogers,' 'ayes,' and a 'light 'em up, boss-man' from the necros. He attached a heavy cable ending in an alligator clamp to the door, sidestepping the sparks as the clamp bit down and completed the circuit. The cable's other end disappeared into the navel of a deader dressed in a day-glo leotard with matching headband, chained to the wall. The dead woman's head turned to follow Jasmine as she walked by.

"Eyes front, Betty," Helgo said, and the deader turned away.

The engine room was a chaotic soup of red, green, and amber lights flashing in their consoles, smoke, ozone, grease-faced necros shouting at each other, and Cyndi Lauper playing on the overhead speakers. The dynamo whined a sour pitch and the floor vibrated in a way she knew wasn't good.

"Snot-boy! You're trying to correct a cable impedance mismatch, not the whole load! Gentle!" Helgo shouted. "Did the captain send you?" he said to Jasmine.

"Not exactly." She gave him the quick version of her trip from the bridge.

"Chevket? Assuming we make it through this, I'll animate that bastard's corpse just to kick him in the balls. Until then, you're with me. That damned pursuit ship's sonic is inducing all kinds of noise on the dynamo. We've already had to eject Weasel and Rob the Knob and jack in the Thompson Twins. Hence, this." He waved a hand at the speakers.

"What can I do to help?" she asked.

"Stand there and call out the numbers for the power output and core temperature every few seconds."

Jasmine stood where he pointed, searching for the proper dials. She ran a finger across the brass nameplates until she found the correct read-outs. The dynamo's power wavered between seventy-five and eighty percent, while the core temperature's needle was already past the green zone and into the yellow. "Seventy-six percent total out, 4,000 and rising."

"Jules, Dammit-Hammer warm up Lemmy and Tripod and stand ready to jack them in. Thompson, cue up some Jackyl and be ready to cut over on transfer."

"They're only good for half-power, boss. They'll burn up unless we cut the load," Thompson said.

"Noted. Mind the board."

Jules and Hammer walked to the deader bank and began moving the pods over to the dynamo on overhead gantries.

Corker swore from the far corner. "Power surge!"

The master power needle jumped. "Output pegged, 4,500...4,700...5,000 and rising fast." The vibration under her feet took on a galloping quality and the dynamo whined like a thousand tortured rats. Purple light shot out from the deader pods.

"Get those deaders ready for cut-over!" Helgo shouted.

Jules and Hammer scrambled as they placed the coffins in empty cradles, slamming latches home and attaching cables with quick twists.

"5,500...6,000...6,700," Jasmine said. "7,000, in the red now!"

"Ready!" Jules called out, quickly echoed by Hammer.

"Dump 'em," Helgo said to Snot-boy. Snot-boy pulled a lever and the floor opened up underneath the dynamo. The Thompson Twins, still glowing, the air shimmering from the heat, tumbled into the open sky leaving only a whiff of char and ozone behind. They dynamo's whine pitched down and the power dropped to zero, the temperature needle receded from red to yellow and back to green. Snot-boy threw the lever forward and the hatches closed.

"Ten seconds until the capacitors fail," Snot-boy said.

"Cue the music, spin it up!" Helgo commanded.

The overhead speakers squealed with guitar and distorted bass drums while the dynamo shuddered with a mechanical clunk and emitted a low growl.

"Power at ten percent, now twenty. It's 750 on the core temp and climbing," Jasmine said.

"Climbing, already? They can't have adapted the jamming yet." Helgo turned to the soundboard. "Thompson?"

"That surge blew my pre-amps, boss-man! Playback is good and fucked."

"Marvelous." Helgo looked to the ceiling and bit his lip, nodding to himself. "Okay, all right then. Fix it, Thompson. The rest of you, we're going direct inject." The necros exchanged glances but headed for the stage and picked up instruments. "Corker, I need you minding the master panel. Snot-boy, time to shine." The apprentice scrambled to the drum set with the others. "Jasmine, can you sing? Yolanda was our vocals."

"Not a note," she said, twisting her bracelets.

Helgo looked like he was ready to spew a litany of curses but held himself in check at the last moment. "Okay. We'll make up for the lost power some other way."

Jasmine looked down and then held out her wrist. "What about these? They're from Bishop's guitar."

Helgo blinked. "The Landweaver?"

"The same. Will they help?"

"They will indeed."

Jasmine slid the strings off her wrist and unraveled them. Helgo ran to his guitar and stripped off two strings while continuing to instruct the other necros.

Her whole arm felt odd, alien. Her wrist burned, and her fingers went numb. She clamped a hand to her wrist and squeezed. Perhaps later she could find some lotion, maybe a bandage.

"Jasmine?" Helgo chucked his chin at the dynamo.

Jasmine shook her head to clear it and glanced at the gauge. "1,800 and climbing. Output's at fifty."

"Capacitors draining, got about a minute before they're empty," Corker said.

"Cut weapons and engine feeds if you need to, but keep those shields fed, Corker."

He re-strung his guitar and twisted the tuning pegs. He cocked an ear and plucked a string, giving the peg a small nudge and quickly repeated the process on the other.

"They're starting to cook, boss-man," Corker said.

"2,000...2,500," Jasmine said. "Power is dropping. Forty-five percent now."

Helgo grabbed a pick and strummed. The note danced over her skin, raising goosebumps. The air seemed cleaner, and the gauge's needle slowed its upward sweep.

"It needs more time to acclimate, but it'll have to do," Helgo said. He turned and slapped hands with the other necros on stage. "We're going pure Cult, guys, starting with 'In the Clouds.' If you screw up, just move on. Snot-Boy, don't rush us, take your cue from Hammer and you'll be fine, okay? Count us down."

Snot-boy cracked his neck then tapped his sticks together. "Two, three, four."

Helgo launched into a buzzsaw guitar riff. Jules nodded along and copied it a measure later on her guitar. Snot-boy gave his drumsticks a twirl and entered with cymbal crash and bass drum kick, taking up the beat. The music slid over Jasmine's skin and tickled her scalp, making her feel as if she could power the dynamo herself. Then Helgo nodded at Hammer who came in on bass like a bulldozer, pushing the band along with him.

The needles on the dynamo jumped, not only the main power but the subsystems as well. The core temp climbed, slowly.

"Main at fifty-two percent, core's at 2,750."

Helgo nodded and skipped over to Jules, and by some telepathy Jasmine couldn't fathom, they both leaned into their riffs, their nodding heads bobbing harder and harder, nearly into a full headbang.

The dynamo picked up speed, somehow humming in tune with the band. The output rose to fifty-five, sixty-five, seventy-five percent and climbed steadily. The core temp needle crept out of the green zone into the yellow.

The tune changed as Helgo's guitar took another melody, layering it over Jules'.

"Subsystems at full power, but I can't throttle down the main," Corker yelled. "We're gonna spike!"

"Shunt the extra to the shields and electros, they can handle it," Helgo said.

Corker leaned into the speaking tube. "Bridge, engine room. You're riding the thunder god for the next sixty seconds. Make it count!"

The main power gauge tipped just past 100 percent, and the smaller gauges for the shield and electro-gun feeds were pegged, off the scale. Helgo launched into a solo and the shadows in the bay faded as the exterior view ports glowed white. There were secondary flashes as a river of plasma balls flowed into the *Immigrant Song*. Electro-guns, rapid-firing. The core temp's needle crept higher, 3,500...3,700.

The solo ended, leaving the bass and drums alone for a few measures and settling the temperature needle. Helgo gave Jules a smile, and she returned it as they hit their rejoin together. The necros settled into a groove, full-on headbanging now and even Jasmine had a hard time focusing on her job, the music infusing her and making her body want to move.

Corker let out a whoop and scrambled out from under his sound board. He flipped a switch and scanned the dials, hands flying across and adjusting knobs. He caught Helgo's eye and gave a thumbs up.

The song began winding down and with it, the dynamo. The main power dropped and held at sixty percent, and the core temp dropped to normal. Corker held up his hands and began counting down the seconds, the others kept an eye on him and brought the song to a close just as Corker's hand closed into a fist. He flipped a switch and scanned the dials before throwing the metal horns.

"That'll hold us for a bit, boss-man."

"How're the deaders?"

"They're a little cooked, but they should recover."

The ship's all-call sounded and Beaumont's voice came through. "Engine room, Bridge. My complements. The boarding party has been repelled and we're free of the trap, but hold at stations until security can complete its sweep for stragglers."

Helgo reached for the tube. "Bridge, engine bay. Acknowledged. We had some help from Miss Shaw and her Badlands juju."

"Miss Shaw? Is she there now?"

Helgo raised his eyebrows, and Jasmine held out her hand for the tube. "I'm here, captain."

"You have my thanks for dealing with the Blood Weeper. Is Chevket with you as well?"

"Chevket was your traitor. He's dead now."

A pause. "Very well. I will await you on the bridge. Please see me at your earliest convenience after we secure from battle stations."

Helgo ran a hand through his hair and let out a breath.

"That bad?" Jasmine said.

"Close enough. We'll probably have to set down to repair all the damage and finesse the dynamo until we get more deaders, but it beats the alternative." He picked up his guitar and tapped at Bishop's strings with reverence. "These are alive," he said. "You felt that, didn't you?'

"I felt something."

"There's no way Lemmy and Tripod should have been able to put out that kind of power, let alone survive it. I can hold my own on guitar but an axe strung with the Landweaver's strings?" He shook his head. "Sweetness. Makes me wonder what I could do with a full set of six and a pair of deaders worth a goddamn." He started unwinding the strings, but Jasmine stopped him.

"Keep them," she said. "They're doing more good here than they are dangling from my wrist."

Helgo looked from her to the guitar, conflicted. "I can't..."

She smiled. "I think Bishop would have wanted–"

A plasma bolt flared past the left-side ports. The ship's all-call whistled.

"New contact! New Contact bearing zero-zero-zero. *Metallica*-class battlecruiser."

"Balls." Helgo put the guitar down. "Now we know who supplied the pursuit ships with extra deaders."

"*Metallica*-class? Did Ryan name those too?"

"You don't want to know the original designation. It involved matriarchal fornication."

"Can the *October Sky* take it?"

Helgo leaned against a post and fished a cigarette out from his front pocket. "Nope." He lit the ciggie and took a long drag. "Battlecruisers have stronger shields, longer range guns, and more of 'em. They also run quad-linked deaders in their engine rooms to power fuck-all. On a good day we could just about outrun them, but today is not a good day." He held out the cigarettes to Jasmine, but she shook her head. He tossed the cigarettes to Jules who arched an eyebrow at him. He shrugged and tossed her the lighter too.

"So what will they do?"

"They can stand off and blow us to hell from a distance, or close to disable and send over boarding parties."

Who's going to take the bullets for you now, Jasmine?

The necros passed the cigarettes around, lighting up and trying to tell jokes. Snot-boy's hand trembled so Dammit lit the cigarette for him. Helgo rubbed a hand over his guitar, tapping Bishop's strings with a sad smile.

The voice in her head was right.

"Helgo, it's me they want. I'll lead them away."

"How?"

"Get Beaumont on the tube. I've got a plan."

BACK IN THE LAUNCH BAY, Helgo swapped out a deader dressed in a checkerboard shirt and thin suspenders for the deader woman with the day-glo leotard. The deader man began whispering "Sisss-taah" almost immediately and Helgo had to chain him to the far wall. The deader woman remained silent and if Jasmine didn't know any better, looked at her chained colleague with disdain until Helgo coaxed her into the engine pod.

"Flock of Seagulls here is a serviceable deader, but if you're crazy enough to do this, I'm sending you out with the best. Black Betty took a few slugs in the Badlands so she's hard to pair but she's the fastest dead bitch in the inventory. She'll give you the speed you'll need."

Betty's filmed eyes stared, impatient.

"Come on, Betty. Jasmine's all right."

"Two minutes to contact," the all-call squawked.

"As soon as I'm clear, get the hell out of here, okay? Nobody's dying today because of me."

Helgo gave his leather cowboy hat a tug and nodded, leaving her hollow. She wanted to throw her arms around Helgo and squeeze, feel the reassurance of him squeezing back, but if she did, she knew she would chicken out. She got into the cockpit instead, giving Helgo a confident smile. He closed the canopy and rapped twice on the glass after latching it. Jasmine started the ornithopter's engine and shook out her hand before grabbing the control stick. The room flooded with light as the doors beneath her opened. She turned and found Helgo already at the cradle release. She placed her other hand on the throttle and nodded. Helgo shoved the lever forward, and Jasmine dropped, her stomach suddenly in her throat. She swallowed, pushing the throttle forward and the stick back, growing heavy in her seat. In the distance, the desert ended and the Anvil Mountains began. The *October Sky* had come so close...

Badlands cursed, Jas.

The *October Sky* looked a lot worse from the outside. Several blackened holes dotted the envelope with one giant hole where the Caliphate gunboat had landed and disgorged its boarding party. The envelope itself looked like a crater-pocked egg, yet nearly all the gun turrets remained and swiveled to the *Metallica* as the *October Sky* adjusted its course. On the bridge, Beaumont, in his purple and aqua naval jacket, regarded her and snapped off a salute. Then the shields intensified, blurring his form behind a thousand glowing motes.

Keep them safe, Bishop.

The *October Sky's* shields kept building like a second sun, and Jasmine could almost feel the music the necros direct-injected. The electros opened up, throwing a rippling wave of plasma at the *Metallica,* itself now shimmering with raised shields. The *October's* guns boomed in rhythmic sequence, sending high explosives hurtling towards the massive ship. The *Metallica's* shields flared as the overcharged plasma bolts and explosive shells converged and then the battlecruiser disappeared as the sky bloomed bright with orange flame and blue lightning.

Maybe she wouldn't need her plan after all.

Then the *Metallica* emerged, unscathed. Guns opened up all along its flanks, dorsal and ventral turrets, even the chin guns jutting out like elephant tusks from the bow. The cannonade and plasma reached the *October Sky* and pushed the airship backwards with each hit. The bright shield dimmed and threatened to disappear entirely before the last shell struck just above the bridge. The concussions shook the air around her and shrapnel peppered her canopy.

The *October Sky* began a lumbering turn to the left. She pushed the throttle all the way forward and banked the 'thopter right.

"Come on, take the bait," she said. "Chase the rabbit."

The *Metallica's* course remained unaltered for a few moments before it swung towards the *October Sky*.

Jasmine let out a string of expletives that would have made Helgo proud. She changed course and aimed for a point just in front of the *Metallica's* bridge, trusting she flew too fast for its gunners. The *Metallica* filled her windscreen, and she could pick out each gun as it swiveled. Electros flared and cannons twinkled, racing out to touch her.

"Come on, Betty!" she shouted over her shoulder.

The shots streaked behind her, and she made out a figure on the bridge with binoculars pressed to their face. She pulled back on the throttle and hoped she wouldn't splatter against the craft's windscreen. The mammoth chin guns swiveled. She made eye contact with the captain, a woman with a close-cropped Annie Lennox look. Jasmine extended a middle finger and pushed the throttle forward before the guns could center on her.

In theory.

In practice, the guns boomed and shells whistled to each side. Their passing buffeted the 'thopter, and it slewed into the zeppelin's shields. She pulled the stick to the side at the last second, skipping off the shield, the 'thopter's frame groaning with stress. She fell, the horizon spinning, the stick like a spastic cat in her hands.

Don't fight it. Coax it.

She kept her grip firm and guided the stick back to center then gently corrected, forcing herself to focus on the spin and not the ground filling her view. The spin slowed, and she gradually leveled out though too damn close to the ground. A dust cloud billowed behind her. She pulled up and tried to get her bearings, searching the sky for the *Metallica*, certain a shell with her name on it would rain down at any moment. She caught a flicker to her right, and moments later sand geysered a few hundred yards before her. She angled away and sacrificed speed to buy herself a little altitude, catching a glint coming from the mountains. She pointed the 'thopter's nose at it and told Betty to hang on.

An orange beam lanced out from the mountains, stabbing through the *Metallica* and vaporizing a sedan-sized hole from bridge to rudder. The beam went out, its wake scarring the sky a lighter blue while the *Metallica's* remains collapsed and disintegrated into confetti.

A cold chill ran through Jasmine, and she pushed the 'thopter's nose down and pulled back on the throttle. The orange beam fired again, super-heating the airspace behind her. She pushed lower as fast as she dared and prayed the ground would be merciful. The beam swung down at her. She flinched, sending the 'thopter into a steep bank. The beam followed, winking out just before a sand dune rose like an ocean wave . She pulled the throttle back and flared the wing fans. Something screamed— it might have been her—and the whole craft shuddered. She hit the ground and bounced two, three, five times before she augered into the dune, turning her world black.

16

The 'thopter looked more like a seat strapped to a random assortment of scrap than a machine. She fished her knapsack out and re-adjusted the sword tucked into her belt. Her head felt fine-ish, unscathed but for a few bruises and the cut re-opening under her eye. The swelling was going down already. Since the broken collar bone, her body seemed to be getting better at fixing her mistakes, though the skin around her wrist remained angry and raw.

She stepped over Black Betty's headband and leotard. The deader must have fallen out or been thrown from the crash, and it amused Jasmine to think maybe she had survived and was walking naked through the desert, perhaps heading back to her home in the Badlands. So long as Betty didn't come back to snack on her, Jasmine didn't mind.

Jasmine hitched the knapsack and set off for the orange beam's source in the distant foothills. The sand wasn't hard to cross, but its constant shifting filled her boots and sapped her strength. Jasmine quickly learned to save her legs by sticking to the rocks jutting from the sand. She also realized that despite all her food stockpiling, she hadn't packed any water.

Stupid.

Night soon fell, and she made her way to one of the larger stone outcroppings before the temperature dropped. She burrowed in and huddled against the rock's bulk, trying to soak in as much residual heat as she could. A black scorpion ran across the ground, and she kicked sand at it. The scorpion scuttled sideways, turning its pincers up at her while backing away. It crawled under a rock and peered back at her, pincers and stinger at the ready.

"Oh cut it out. I'm not going to hurt you." She kicked more sand at it, but only a few grains reached its dull carapace. The bug lifted a claw as if warding off the blast and snapped it in agitation.

"I was just minding my own business, you know," she said. "You're the one invading my territory. Whole damn desert out here, plenty of space."

The scorpion kept inching forward, clicking its claw at her.

"It would be so damn easy to kill you, dumb scorpion, pissing off the wrong woman on the wrong day. Do you know who I am?"

The scorpion retreated.

"Damn right," she said. She felt a bit better. Finally, something in this place feared her.

Nothing but rocks and sand here, yet life found a way. Then again, the scorpion could be part of Ryan's meddling too—a mind fragment expressed as little poisonous bug. A stray nasty thought generated among millions in the brain every day, except here those stray thoughts became... things. It made one person a living god: a god with a leaky imagination, stray thoughts, and a tendency to act without thinking. Or worse, a god who spent the last minutes of his mundane teenage life lying in a crumpled heap along the roadside. It was inevitable Ryan would make spectacular mistakes. Maybe it was inevitable she would descend into the same depravity and indifference. She wasn't built for power.

She found herself rubbing her wrist, and her skin itched like ants were picking her apart. She dumped her knapsack out and tossed the food and clothes aside until she found the deader serum. She didn't need a full dose, maybe just a little to numb things.

And then what?

And then she'd be high in the middle of the desert, assuming she didn't OD. That would be bad. The phantom ants on her skin doubled. Fuck it, she was going to take a little.

She plunged the needle through the bottle's rubber seal, drew the cloudy fluid, brought the needle to her arm, and felt its bite as she missed her vein. Cursing, she pulled it out and groped for the cord wrapped around her spare clothes, soon tying off her upper arm and making the veins in her forearm swell. There. She couldn't miss. She wiped away the trickle of blood from her failed attempt and something caught her eye. At her feet, the blood-spattered sand clumped and writhed. She danced back as it solidified into another scorpion this one a translucent white. The black one backed away at an angle, holding its claws wide and wavering between Jasmine and this new threat.

Jasmine looked from the syringe to the scorpion.

"Fuck me," she whispered.

She grabbed a rock and brought it down on the white scorpion with a wet crunch. She twisted the rock a couple times and when she brought it up, the scorpion's carapace slowly unwound into a wet spot on the sand.

She smashed the needle and the serum as well, scattering the pieces.

The black scorpion ran under its boulder and disappeared. Jasmine tossed the rock aside.

"You are so fucking lucky, buddy."

SHE NEEDED WATER. Her thoughts rambled as she trudged closer to the hills. Memories circled around and doubled back on themselves until everything came together in sharp focus.

What would Cally do?

Cally was dead. Cally would have holed up in Paradise City or traveled forever on the *October Sky,* safe. Jasmine wanted more; it wasn't enough to survive. Therefore, she could no longer trust Cally's instincts. Cally was dead.

What a great friend you are, Jas.

She let out a long breath and shook her head to clear it.

This place had to have an exit to an actual heaven, and she needed to take Ryan with her before he pulled it all down around their heads.

Death. He deserves death.

She pushed the thought aside and watched the porpoise-shaped clouds, swirling and being pulled to the sea, The Maw, as Beaumont called it. She felt pulled there too, though she couldn't say why.

Because you're dehydrated and delusional.

Was she? She crested the next dune, taking heart that she was maybe less than a day away from the foothills, and Ryan.

You mean our rapist who shoots airships out of the sky without warning.

"Shut up, me," she muttered.

I will not shut up. We have a second chance at life and you're fucking it up.

And what did she have to show for the afterlife?

A dead not-quite boyfriend, a dead not-quite best friend, and bodies, bodies everywhere.

Mostly at the hands of a psycho samurai who was as much Ryan's victim as anyone. They were all victims, really, all tearing each other apart because of Ryan.

And you too, darling.

And if she was being honest, her too. She stopped as a thought came to her.

No. Hell no.

He was a victim too.

That's no excuse for what he did.

She had blood on her hands too. If there wasn't any hope for Ryan, could there be any for her?

It's different for us, and you know it. We were forced.

She wasn't going to kill Ryan. Not if there was still a way to help him.

Forget it, I'm out of here.

Her whole world shifted, and for a moment she was an alien inside her own skin. The sensation faded, and she blinked as she found herself rubbing her wrist.

Maybe I'm more dehydrated than I thought, huh?

There was no response.

PART III

17

Metal bits coated the foothills from flakes twinkling in the sand to jagged fist-sized chunks lurking in the tall grass. Occasionally, she came across large pits with blackened outlines or pockmarked clearings reeking of chlorine and rust. She kept reminding herself to straighten up, she was surely too small a target for the orange beam and hopefully close enough to Utopia to be met with questions rather than shooting.

She thought about rummaging around her knapsack for the millionth time but knew all she would find was a dried-out biscuit, a bit of salted meat, and a change of clothes. After days of hiking through the desert, her head pounded and her tongue felt grafted to her jaw. Her whole body ached for water. Part of her wondered if destroying the deader serum was wise, if she wouldn't wish for it at the end. The other part shivered at the thought of her comatose body being picked apart by scorpions.

Past the chemical fields, the vegetation was a strange mix of living and dead. Tree trunks up to fifty feet were either charred or bleached white. Their branches ended in jagged edges, though a few had been clean-cut. The new growth held green, tall grass, hardy scrub brush, and whip-like trees just a few feet taller than herself. If plants grew here, that meant water. She ran her swollen tongue across her lips and set about to find some.

When she reached the first stream, she wanted to wail. The tea-colored water rushed over rocks stained orange like a Technicolor nightmare. She couldn't see the streambed's bottom, though it was only a few inches deep. She plunged her hand in cool water that felt soapy under her fingertips. Her hand came out stained orange and carried an acrid tang reminding her of lawn mowers crossed with the ironworks around Gary, Indiana. Still, as she watched the droplets fall from her fingertips, she could fool herself thinking they were clear, and the urge to catch a few with her tongue was overwhelming. She stood and turned her back on the water.

She followed the stream up, its gurgling taunting her the entire way. Some said torture was hearing running water when you had to pee. Not true. She would gladly have endured Niagara Falls on three pots of coffee rather than this. She put the thought to the side and kept walking, mindful for the odd metal bits sharp enough to tear through her boots.

The stream cut its way through the foothills with spindly pine trees eking by at the water's edge. Other, taller trees at least had the good sense to grow on the valley walls. The weeds and waxy scrub she passed had a yellowish hue to their leaves with orange water spots.

She had followed the stream for a few hours when she rounded a bend and let out a gasp. Before her was a logjam of metal limbs: arms, legs, hands and feet, square torsos and dented spheres. Packed between were tank treads, wheels, engines, wires, and bent shapes that had been melted, blasted, or in some cases, torn apart, interlocking as if placed by mechanical beavers. The water seeped over and through the metal, wearing at corroded edges and coating every surface with orange slime.

Six insect-like limbs rose over thirty feet from the lake's middle like a macabre crown. Two joints had rusted off and fallen into the water, leaning against a metal skull the size of a house.

"Fucking robots, Ryan? Robots?"

18

———

Jasmine had hoped the water upstream would clear, but it remained tea-colored and littered with junked robot parts as far as she could see. Svelte winged forms and utilitarian boxes on tank treads; heads with demonic scowls, chrome ovoids, cubes with cyclopic visors, and one with an angelic face and Sputnik-like aerials for hair. All had been weaponized in some way, with guns, rockets, or cannons both integrated and crudely bolted on. A few carried what looked like oversized hand weapons, rifles ten feet long, and chunky pistols big as cinder blocks. The forms repeated, but not a single one remained intact.

Whatever their conflict, they had all ended up in the same place. With one last look at the giant skull's rusty crown, she went deeper into the valley.

Jasmine nibbled at her last biscuit as she walked, the lumps pasty in her mouth and hard to swallow. It wasn't enough to keep her going, and she wondered if she could eat the leaves on the trees or chew them for the liquid. Her first and only attempt lasted five seconds; the acrid after-taste remained for an hour.

There weren't any other robot heaps for the next hour, though their former parts (bones, organs?) crunched under her feet. She stopped that line of thought and kept walking. If she could only find the water's source! History class made it sound so simple. Some explorer or other became the first to discover a river's headwaters. She imagined bearded men with coonskin caps in birchbark canoes just paddling along until they couldn't go any further upstream. It didn't sound hard at all, something done on a weekend or along the way to some other job.

It wasn't even impressive. What's the big deal? You find some little spring or something and then what? Drink from it? Spit in it? Take a leak? Guys were always peeing in the woods. Some way of marking their territory. Maybe that was it. They wanted to find the headwaters and piss in them, so they could claim everything the river touched. She wondered if she would have to go all the way to this stream's headwaters to find something to drink, and if someone had already pissed in it.

LATER THAT AFTERNOON, she had to climb over a tree-sized metal arm. She wondered if its owner lay in the next ravine over, or if it had found somewhere else to die and if she should find something unique to mark its place in case she ran into the robot later. Yes, if she met a two-hundred foot robot with a missing arm, she would absolutely tell it where its arm was. Then maybe it wouldn't squish her. Part of her thought that was funny, but she was too tired to smile.

She rounded a bend and found the lake, its near shore the same orange-brown as the stream but deep blue at the far end. Her hopes rose as did the urge to run and gorge on the water, only her legs wouldn't accept anything faster than a walk. With her luck, she would probably impale herself on a rusty shard in the weeds. No, check that, she would scratch herself and die slowly from tetanus. Nothing in this world wanted her to die quickly. So she forced her thirst to the side and watched her feet, making sure they weren't going to condemn her by either fast or slow method.

Lush pines on the far side reflected in the deep blue water, like one of those perfect little lakes promised in Northwoods cabin brochures, vintage beer advertisements, and slasher movies. Of course, the rest of the lake with its brown water and apocalyptic metal skeletons breaching the surface would scare away tourists, sportsmen, and horny teenagers alike.

She almost stumbled when she reached clean water. Rusty algae blooms just below the surface marked the border, swaying under the faster current emptying into the lake. Her body overrode her control and she ran to the shore's edge, past the blooms to where the stream entered the lake. She fell to her knees and scooped water into her mouth.

She tried to sip at the water, but the first swallow made her want more. Her hands plunged into the cold lake and she brought her face to the water's surface, nearly to the tip of her nose. She scooped up handful after handful, gulping each as fast as she could before surrendering and dunking her head under the surface.

She came up choking while her body wrestled with the urges for both water and air. The back of her throat hurt like it had cracked, despite swallowing half the lake. She went down for another drink but stopped herself, remembering from some TV show that people stranded in the desert got sick from drinking too much water at once because their bodies weren't used to it. Her stomach turned a bit at this thought, and she pushed herself away. The last thing she needed was hurling up the water her body needed.

She lay back on the bank and rested. She thought the water would be the sweetest taste ever, like how stale potato chips were a gourmet delight to a starving man, but she didn't remember anything except filling her stomach. On the whole, maybe it was good she hadn't noticed the taste. It probably meant the water was clean. Yes, she would believe this because it was too late to change anything now.

She looked into the sky and said, "Let the record note that should I get sick from drinking this water, it was not a good idea." She laughed to herself, a dry cackle ending in a coughing fit.

"Probability of death from ingestion less than from particle beam," a flat voice said.

Jasmine rolled over and couldn't figure out where the voice had come from until the boulder beside her moved. Sandstone coloring seemed to melt and its outline broke up over the next second until a robot in mottled tan and black stood over her. It reminded her of the Rock 'Em Sock 'Em robot game Ryan got one Christmas. Squarish head, broad shoulders, and long arms. The mottling across its surface mimicked limestone perfectly, though on its chest the blobs came together to form the number 147 like a name tag.

For the next few moments, she couldn't speak. When her voice decided to work again, the first words from her mouth were, "So the water is okay?"

The robot's head remained motionless while it motors let out a high-pitched whine as it swiveled the rest of its body around, ready to walk away from her. A camera-like lens on the left side and an offset quarter-sized silver circle on its right made it seem as if it looked at her cockeyed. "Irrelevant. We must go now before the Mega returns. Follow."

"I'm not going anywhere. Too tired."

"Imperative. You must follow, or the Mega will exterminate you."

She didn't know what a mega was, or what this robot was either. It probably had something to do with all the rusting carcasses out here, the big orange airship-vaporizing beam, or something really deep and complex. She didn't care. Life was pretty simple right now. She had water, and she was spent. The apocalypse could come falling down around her, and she wouldn't be able to move a muscle.

Jasmine said, "I couldn't possibly go another step. If you want me to leave, you'll have to carry me."

Its body pivoted back around, still eerily keeping its head motionless. "Confirmed." It reached out and picked her up with a surprising gentleness. It rose to full height on pistoned legs bent the wrong way like an ostrich's and bounded along the shoreline, then into the woods. She watched pine boughs pass by overhead and let her body rock from side to side with each step. The apocalypse would wait, she thought, and she fell asleep.

19

———

Jasmine woke up on a cot under a fluorescent light. She felt hollow. She turned her head and found herself staring at a yellow plastic sign showing a stick figure slipping on wavy black lines. The sign leaned against a bucket with a mop handle reaching nearly to the ceiling. Since the mop appeared to be normal size, Jasmine figured she would have to watch her head when she got up. Not that she would be stirring anytime soon. Her whole body had the muscle tone of an old dish cloth, and she had the feeling that something was missing. Her hand went to her wrist and twisted naked skin. Her bracelet was gone. That must have been it.

The problem was she was tired, but not sleepy. Given the choice between counting the avocado tiles on the walls and calling out for help, she cleared her throat. The door opened, and the robot stuck its head in the cramped space, making Jasmine feel like a toy in a dollhouse.

"That was quick," she said, "You weren't standing outside this whole time, were you?"

"You needed rest and supervision. I had no other tasks to perform."

"So you stuck me in the broom closet and waited for me to wake up."

"Sub Dormitory 1-A," it said. "Its primary purpose is to provide individual rejuvenation for biologicals."

She looked around at the walls and nodded at the mop. "It's a closet."

"It is a dormitory that happens to have a mop," it said.

She put her head back against the cot and threw an arm over her eyes. "Whatever. How long have I been sleeping?"

"Fifteen hours, thirty-nine minutes."

"I'm hungry," she said, blurting it out as soon as it occurred to her. That would explain the hollowness, too.

"Food is available in Cafeteria Five."

She laughed. "What's wrong with one through four?"

"Empty, corrupted, infested, and irradiated; in that order. Are you able to move independently, or shall I access the feeding pastes?"

She raised her arm up a bit to block the glare and peer at the robot through one eye. If it had been human it would have been able to interpret her look perfectly and know, dammit, just bring her some real food already. The only reaction from the robot was a slight rotation of the camera lens on its left side. It probably couldn't conceive of any other alternatives. After a few moments she sighed and rolled off the cot into a crouch. Her body was one mass of bruises and knots, but she wasn't going to find out how feeding paste tasted.

She walked down the corridors leaning on the robot for support. The ceiling was low, maybe seven feet tall, making the robot hunch down and duck walk to keep from scraping its head on the fluorescent lamps that illuminated as they approached. The place seemed like a cross between a hospital and bomb shelter. Color-coded parallel lines on the floors and walls met and departed at each intersection. Some lines ended at solid metal doors with little glass and wire mesh windows, always dark on the other side. When she asked the robot once what was behind one of the doors, it only said 'Office A-Twenty-Three,' which agreed with the placard mounted to the side. When further pressed, it admitted it didn't know anything else about the room.

Questions bubbled in her mind, but she put them aside. Food, water, rest. Everything else could wait.

The cafeteria could feed hundreds. Jasmine sat in a corner at the end of a long table eating canned peaches with a white plastic fork—a fitting dessert to the military-style lasagna ration the robot had provided. There was a peculiar delight in feeling the fruit's flesh yield and slide down her throat. Thick syrup dripped off her chin, and she wiped at it with the back of her hand. She licked the remains off her wrist almost without thinking, not wanting any going to waste. She sat back and placed her hands on her belly, full for the first time in days. There are so few indulgences as satisfying as eating, she thought, and she resolved to become fat someday. Maybe that's why the only laughing Buddha was a fat one. The thin ones were too serious.

The robot had stayed quiet and still while she ate. The camouflage pattern faded to a dull gray color with the same "147" label on its chest.

"I take it you're called one-four-seven," she said.

The robot rose to full height, about twelve feet. "I am Hades model general infantry unit designated GIU-147. I have been known by many names, one-four-seven being the most common."

"I'll call you Spot."

"I shall respond to the name Spot."

"Just like that?" Jasmine shook her head. "What if I wanted to call you Gossamer instead?"

"I would respond to Gossamer, or Spot, as you designate."

"What makes me so special?"

"You are the biological," it said.

"So you'll do what I say?"

"Within parametrically-defined limits."

Jasmine didn't know what to make of that. She knew she should be sharper, but her thoughts felt so clumsy. She needed to get her bearings. "Okay, Spot. Where are we?"

"We are in Utopia Vault Seven."

"Utopia? You mean like the city of Utopia?"

"Correct."

"Ah," Jasmine said, scraping the can's sides with her fork. "Now we're getting somewhere. So tell me what the hell happened here, why I had to step over rusted metal ever since I left the desert." She put the fork in her mouth and set her tongue probing for the last bits of sweet syrup.

"The city-state of Utopia was a perfect society until it ceased functioning shortly after the schism."

"What exactly was this "schism"?"

"Analysis indicates a literal versus metaphorical interpretation of certain philosophical texts."

"So it was a religious war?"

Servos whined as it shook its head. "Inconclusive, though Utopia was founded as a secular community. The biologicals that later manufactured me only agreed on the schism contributing to destructive events."

Jasmine glanced around the empty room. "Are there any other biologicals here?"

"No."

She stared at the robot for several moments. "They're all dead, aren't they?" she said.

"Yes."

But not Ryan. The fight with the Blood Weeper proved that. "How many?"

"411 biologicals and 630,503 mechanicals have been rendered inoperative."

The way it said "inoperative" jarred her. It wasn't like those people could ever be fixed, nor the robots unless Spot knew how to do it.

"Do you know Ryan Shaw? Maybe called the Creator?"

"Ryan Shaw is the founding citizen of Utopia."

"Is he still here?"

"You are the only biological in Utopia."

"So he must have left at some point. I'm sure he's still alive somewhere."

"I have no record of his departure. Logic suggests he is missing and likely dead."

"How could you not know, didn't he rule here?"

"Ryan Shaw called himself a citizen and then declared that all citizens are equal."

Jasmine shook her head. "Someone had to be in charge."

"Utopia was created by 1,747 mechanicals under biological citizen oversight. Each citizen proposed and voted on ideas. The collective population directly controlled Utopia; mechanicals executed its collective will."

"But it didn't work out well in the end. Did the humans and mechanicals fight each other, like a civil war?" Hadn't Ryan learned anything from *The Terminator*?

"No, they died fighting the Megas."

"What the hell is a Mega?"

"The Megas were designed to provide defense from foreign elements. They stood one hundred feet tall, equipped with heavy armor and an advanced particle projectile cannon plus other munition delivery systems."

She reached for a canned juice, which Spot opened by punching its fingers through the metal lid. "What happened?" she asked.

"The collective will directed the Megas to quell civil unrest, subtype riot."

"This is the schism?"

"Logic suggests. Records around this time contain irregularities. The vote resulted in orders were either flawed or sabotaged and all biologicals were tagged hostile. Thousands were rendered inoperable by the time the collective mounted a defense. All citizens, slaves, and mechanicals fought the Megas. I was the last unit manufactured before the fabricators went offline."

"And how many Megas were there?"

"Four. The city destroyed three, with significant losses. You passed one Mega's remains already."

Jasmine remembered the lake, the dam made of robots, and the gargantuan metal skull in the middle. The robot nodded when she said this.

"One unit remains operable, attacking any biological or mechanical entity it encounters."

"It's the one shooting down airships."

"Affirmative."

"So how do we get past it?"

"Irrelevant," it said.

"Pardon?"

The robot spread its arms with a jerk. "This vault contains consumables sufficient for your estimated lifespan." It brought its arms back to its sides abruptly. "We shall remain here."

"I don't think so," Jasmine said. "I'm not spending the rest of my life living like a mole."

"You must. If you go outside, the Mega or other environmental factors will render you inoperative. Staying here is the optimal choice."

"Not for me. I have things to do. Ryan is out there somewhere." She eyed the robot, wondering how fast it could move.

"Facial and breathing patterns suggest a high probability of fight-or-flight instinct. I assure you I am here to protect you and ensure your survival."

"Yeah, I'm sure. I'm not anyone's prisoner, okay?"

Spot remained silent.

"Look, Spot, let's say I do stay here and live for another seventy or eighty years. I still die alone in the end. Then what?"

The robot remained silent.

"You don't know, do you?"

"Irrelevant."

Jasmine threw the peach can at it. It bounced off the robot's head and clattered to the floor. The robot didn't move. Jasmine got up and turned to walk out. Something was wrong with her eyes. The room seemed lost in a fog. Her head felt like it was filling with sand. Memories of the *hareem*. No, she thought to herself, get out. She tried to move her legs and felt herself fall. Something grabbed her arms.

When her eyes cleared, heat swept through her and sweat prickled her scalp. She was looking up at the robot. In its camera-eye's reflection her face was flushed and her eyes showed white all around.

"Blood pressure event," the robot said. "You lost consciousness momentarily when you changed elevations."

"You mean when I stood up."

"I mean when you stood up," it said.

"I'm not staying here."

"Irrelevant. You cannot leave while your body recovers function."

A smile crossed her lips. "So I can leave once I get better."

It paused in thought, or at least didn't respond while something inside its body whirred and ticked for a few seconds. "You cannot leave while your body recovers function."

An argument for another time. "Fine. If you would please help me back to a cot or bed, I think I want to sleep."

20

---

asmine awoke to the echo of her screams. Spot stood motionless at the end of her cot, its left camera eye whirring.

"REM sleep interrupted," it said in its monotone voice.

"It's called a nightmare," Jasmine said. "There was this giant flying bug except it was also a deader trying to find me and when I turned around—ugh, I need a drink."

"There is a water bottle under the cot," Spot said.

"I don't want water, I want a drink. Wine, liquor, I'll even have a beer if that's the only thing available."

"There are no alcoholic beverages in Utopia."

"Then it's no utopia."

"Semantic type mismatch. Ignored."

Jasmine got up and went to the mirror. Her hair was greasy, but hell with it, Spot wouldn't care. She could stay here forever with her own personal robot and never worry again. Then she remembered the scorpions and shivered.

"Are the environmental settings out of parametric bounds?" Spot asked. "This unit will adjust settings and recover a sweater for use in the intervening lag."

"Huh?" she blurted, then shook her head. "No, I was thinking of something else. The temperature's fine."

Spot's head tilted, as if considering, or like a confused dog. "Involuntary reaction to emotional event. Searching for solution." Spot's head straightened. "You need to relax."

Jasmine snorted. "I'm working on it."

"Confirmed. Biological stress markers down two point eleven percent since first encounter. Estimate return to acceptable levels in 117 days, variant on post-traumatic stress and latent depressive state manifestations."

"You can read my mood?" Jasmine said, suddenly not feeling as safe as she once had.

"Confirmed. Mood state estimate updated: 121 days."

"Stop that."

"Confirmed." Spot paused then added. "You need to relax."

"Keep saying that and see what happens to my mood state."

"Acknowledged."

"Acknowledged?" She narrowed her eyes at it.

"Confirmed."

"That's better."

~

SHE WALKED through the door labeled "Cafeteria storage facility #5-AA1," a fancy label for the storeroom next to the cafeteria's dishwasher. Spot followed, clomping on rubberized treads with hydraulic pops and servo whines. The lights came on automatically, illuminating a concrete room filled with stacked white plastic crates. Each crate was stenciled with a label in black ink detailing the variety and quantity of meal ration contained within. She walked a few feet down and stopped at a crate labeled STEW, BEEF QTY 100. She slipped a foiled packet into her knapsack. As she went along the aisle, she added PASTA, PRIMAVERA; ENCHILADA, CHICKEN; COBBLER, PEACH (along with its cousins APPLE and CHERRY); and HASH, SOUTHWEST (MILD).

"Where's the jambalaya?" she asked.

A laser flashed from Spot's shoulder, sweeping out across all the crates in less than a second and stopping at an upper shelf.

She dropped the backpack, pulled herself up on the lowest shelf, and began looking for another handhold.

"Cease. Desist. Unacceptable risk," Spot said.

"What? I'm just going to climb up there and drop a few pouches down. I'll be fine."

"Ascending above six feet without safety harness prohibited."

"Do you have a safety harness?"

Spot's laser swept out through the room again. "Negative."

"Well I'm not going to miss out on jambalaya. Catch me if I fall."

"Negative. Ascent prohibited." It closed its three-fingered claw hand around her ankle in a gentle grip. She shook her leg but it was useless, Spot didn't budge.

"I will retrieve the jambalaya," it said.

"You're too heavy to climb the shelves."

"Confirmed. I will use the forklift."

"Oh. Right. I'm coming down, then."

Spot released her and emitted a trilling sound like an old dial-up modem. Moments later, a forklift emerged from a hidden door and maneuvered itself to get the crate down under Spot's direction.

Jasmine stood back and let them work, stretching and rubbing a knot at the back of her neck. She needed to move, she was getting soft. Though these past days had been restful, she couldn't stay. She could feel something tugging at her—The Maw. Even underground she could reach out and point to it.

"Objective secure," Spot announced and handed her a jambalaya packet.

Jasmine stuffed it in her knapsack and swung it on her back. "That ought to be enough."

"Query: is securing foodstuffs in mobile storage unit increasing your operating efficiency?"

Jasmine hesitated. Spot had grabbed her because she had the gall to try climbing up a shelf. She had let her guard down around the robot—a mistake. Just because it took orders from her didn't mean it would do everything she said.

"Why yes, Spot. This way, I won't have to walk all the way down to the cafeteria if I become injured."

“This unit would retrieve the required foodstuffs.”

“What if you’re inoperable?”

“Acknowledged. Securing of foodstuffs for this scenario increases survivability.”

“I knew you’d see it my way.” She had another idea. “Now do you have a medical bay? I want to familiarize myself with its layout.”

21

———

The medical bay's drab blue-green walls matched the floor tiles which really set off the corroded plate-sized drains set every ten feet. Dozens of rolled-up mattresses rested at the foot of black metal-framed beds arranged in double rows separated by white night-stands. If the robots hadn't killed people outright, they probably died soon after with hospitals like this. Jasmine put the queasy feeling in her stomach aside and pushed through a set of doors leading into a hallway. They passed operating rooms in which machines hunched over tables like insects with sickles and drills for arms.

"Are those surgical robots?" she asked.

"Unknown function type. The units appear to be without power. Shall I reactivate them?"

"No." She had enough nightmares already, thank you. She moved on until she found a promising room: an examination table, a desk, and many sets of drawers. She rummaged through the drawers, occasionally setting aside syringes, bandages, and sample tubes.

Spot cocked its head as she worked. "Analysis inconclusive. Query: what are you doing?"

Jasmine found the rubbing alcohol. "I need to take blood samples."

"I am not programmed to take blood samples."

She rummaged around another drawer until she found a small length of tubing with needles at either end. "Neither am I but I've seen it done." Actually, she always looked away at the doctor's office when they took blood samples, but she would figure it out.

It turned out harder than she expected. Spot refused to poke her with a needle so she had to do it herself. Her arm ached from her botched attempts at finding a vein though Spot did eventually help hold her arm down. She ended up filling a dozen pinky-sized tubes, sealed and slotted in a plastic case like little soldiers.

"What tests will you perform?" Spot asked.

"Pathogen, tox screen, hemoglobin count that kind of thing."

"Stress sensors indicate falsehood in your statement."

Shit. "I'm not lying," she lied. "Well, okay, I don't know how to do those tests right now but maybe I'll find a book on how to do it." Emphasis on *maybe*.

Spot said nothing.

Jasmine frowned at the scattered medical trash. "What should I do about all this?"

"A maintenance droid will remove all refuse after we leave."

"What do they look like?"

"Your behavior patterns suggest it would be better to withhold this information."

"You're not telling me?"

"This unit suggests your mental function would be less impaired if you voluntarily end this inquiry vector."

"Just 'suggests,' so if I order you?"

"I would comply."

"Then I so order you."

Spot let out a digital chirp and in the hallway, a panel opened. A metal-on-metal scratching within the walls sent a shiver down her spine. Through the door came a two-foot long mottled bronze cockroach, antennae quivering. Jasmine yelped as the thing scuttled past them and leapt onto the counter, pushing medical waste into its mouthparts with a high-pitched buzzing coupled with a low droning as gleaming instruments simultaneously shred and sucked the waste into its body.

Jasmine had the short sword in hand, chisel-tip pointed at the droid while she tried to breathe.

Spot's camera eye whirred. "*Wakizashi*, traditional short sword of the samurai. Part of the *daishō* when paired with the *katana*."

The sword—*wakizashi*, she corrected herself—seemed alive. It hummed in her hand, waiting for release. "Those things come out when we're not around?"

"Affirmative"

"In the dark?"

"Affirmative."

"How—" She swallowed and forced herself to calm down. "How many are there in this bunker?"

"Inquiry: is this an order?"

"Are you saying I don't want to know?"

"Affirmative."

"Then let's get out of here." The waste droid let out a digital chirp and gathered itself to jump down when Spot chirped back and froze it in place. Unfortunately, it faced Jasmine with something red glistening on a mandible and the droid, somehow sensing it, began cleaning it with two smaller mouthparts.

Jasmine ran through the med bay not stopping until she reached the main hallway. Perhaps Ryan had gotten something right about health care in Utopia because she was damned sure not going back in there again. And from now on, she'd sleep with a light on.

22

The next few days quickly organized themselves into a routine. She would wake up and find Spot waiting to escort her to the cafeteria for breakfast. Then they would walk the vault's dead corridors to help her regain strength. She hadn't quite gotten used to the endless hallways with their 70s color palette and 50s paranoia vibe. The wood-paneled doors were generically labeled and always locked. Spot refused to open them, citing her lack of need versus potential future residents. Jasmine spent most of their walks trying to convince the robot of a logical need but was thwarted each time by a polite counter.

Her footsteps echoed in the corridors in counterpoint to Spot's heavy tread. Jasmine went over her mental list of reasons to let her go and tried to think of a new one that might convince the robot. As they wandered through an unexplored wing, the lights revealed an opportunity.

The hallway ended in a set of double steel doors outlined in yellow and black hazard stripes. Black stenciled letters identified the room as ARMORY 1A.

"Let's go in there," she said.

Spot said, "No. Weapons are not needed within the living quarters."

Maybe she should stop asking for permission. "Yes, but I'm not going to stay in the living quarters much longer, I'm well enough to go outside now." She stopped and raised her chin. "I'm going outside."

"New objective noted, updating response model." The robot stopped and swiveled to face her. "Negative. You will remain here and repopulate Utopia."

She put a hand on the *wakizashi.* "I will *not,*" she said, her face hot. Before Spot could update her "days until acceptable stress levels" estimate, she put a finger in its camera. "Don't."

Spot remained silent.

"Anyway, I'm all alone here. Nobody is getting pregnant."

"Acknowledged."

"Acknowledged? Not confirmed?"

"There are numerous aircraft approaching our coordinates, should they land, there is a high probability of male subjects with suitable genetic diversity."

"As much as I'm thrilled a robot is planning my male harem, I have to pass."

"Moderate probability of other females. Breeding responsibilities would be shared among population to ensure optimal use of resources for use in rebuilding civilization."

"Since when was that your responsibility?"

"Spot's programming implies such action."

"And who would be in charge?"

"To be determined."

Jasmine shook her head. "It's not happening. I will not lie around for the rest of my days and pop out babies so forget about rebuilding Utopia. I so order it."

Spot lurched as her words hit it. A moment later it recovered and chimed.

"Recommended action: recalculate parameters and rescind previous order."

"No."

"Recalculate parameters and rescind previous order."

"I said no, now stop it. Don't make me order you again."

"Acknowledged," Spot said after a moment. Jasmine wondered if the pause was programmed petulance or some deeper thinking on its part. This was the third time Spot claimed she would remain underground. She wondered if she could keep on using the brute force of her orders to get her way or if the robot would eventually outsmart her.

"Wait a minute, airships approaching? Won't they get shot down by that orange beam?" She prayed Beaumont had the good sense to run after seeing what happened to the *Metallica*, but she realized she couldn't discount the Caliphate or Paradise City ignoring the risk and continuing their hunt for her.

"The Mega's particle projector cannon will destroy all incoming aircraft with a ninety-seven percent probability."

"I still don't see how that suddenly gives you an opportunity to play matchmaker with a new group of humans if the Mega is going to get them first."

"This unit did specify the qualifier 'should they land.' Probability of total destruction decreases with every landing attempt and new strategies implemented. Estimating a fifty percent chance of viable match within the decade based on historical trends."

"Well, I'm going to be long gone before they succeed, once I find out where my brother went."

"Acknowledged."

"Hmph." She looked back at the doors and had an idea. "If we destroyed the Mega, or disabled it, the ships would have a higher survival probability. Agreed?"

"Confirmed."

"And that would hold greater promise than letting Paradise City and the Caliphate send people to die over the generations?"

It stood silent for several moments internal fans turned on and vented excess heat from Spot's CPU housing. "Confirmed," it finally responded.

"To do that, I will need to go outside. If I'm going outside, I need to protect myself."

"This unit will protect you."

"That's nice, Spot, but what if something happens to you? I will be left defenseless." She pointed to the doors. "In there are things that would increase my chances of survival in that case."

"Probability low," said Spot.

"Probability higher with a weapon than without."

"Probability unknown, extrapolating." Spot looked to the armory and a red light shot out from its shoulder to the door, flashing over a bar code, then disappeared. Spot stood still for several moments, silent.

"So are we going in or not?" Jasmine said.

Spot made a high-pitched chirp. The armory doors groaned, then opened as long unused gears engaged cogs.

"Cool," Jasmine said. "Let's go."

Spot's arm rose to block her way. "Caution. This armory's weapons catalog lists several systems unsuitable for biological mounting. This unit will designate which systems are acceptable."

A row of lights beyond the armory doors came on, illuminating racks upon racks holding rifles, missiles, cannons, and at the far edges, bizarre shapes she couldn't put names to. She didn't know how big the armory was, but she had the impression it could outfit a small army.

"Right," she said. "Look, but don't touch. I got it. Let's go shopping."

She found herself expecting a sarcastic thought that never came.

"How about this one?" Jasmine said. She held a gleaming rifle as big around as a telephone pole. The jagged edges below the muzzle looked like it could skewer a rhino.

"ATLAS MK17 unit—portable plasma projector cannon. Primary use: engaging heavily armored ground targets and aircraft," Spot said. "Unacceptable."

"Why?" Jasmine said. "Sounds like just what I need." If she was fighting a giant robot, she wanted the biggest damn weapon she could carry.

"The system masses forty-seven point five percent of your body weight, and does not include the necessary power unit."

"Well how much would that weigh?"

"An additional twenty kilos, for the basic pack. It would provide enough energy for five discharges."

Twenty kilos, a bit less than forty-five pounds, and that was just the battery. Jasmine hoisted the weapon back into its cradle.

"So what would you recommend, Spot?"

A red laser swept out from the robot's shoulder and over each rack's barcode as it walked between them. Jasmine followed, catching glimpses of barrels the size of trees, bullets as big as her thigh, and at least one chainsaw that would give a sequoia nightmares. As they went farther into the shadows, the guns gave way to bombs and missiles, then to pods bristling with barrels and lenses. Jasmine felt smaller with each step. That hollow feeling returned and she found herself rubbing her wrist.

Spot stopped and turned at an empty rack. Jasmine slid on a grease spot or oil slick—she couldn't tell which—and barked her shin on the rack.

"Dammit, is there anything even here, or are you just stalling?"

Spot crouched down, servo motors whining. Its hand closed around something in the shadows.

"JA-934 Helix," said Spot. "Light infantry weapons system. Experimental." It turned and held the weapon out to her. She couldn't make out much, just an outline of a shoulder stock attached to three bundled tubes.

"It's ugly," she said.

"Irrelevant. This system is the optimal choice for a biological with your training."

"I don't have any training," she said.

"Confirmed."

Jasmine sighed. "So what does it do?"

Spot walked past her back towards the armory entrance. "Follow. I will instruct you in its use."

Spot led her to a room behind another steel door. This one had been marked LABORATORY 7D. Spot opened a tall olive green locker, retrieving a blue steel cylinder and ear plugs. The cylinder fit into the rifle's stock.

"The Helix was designed to test post-civilization battle assumptions."

"You mean it was designed to work if everything went to hell," Jasmine said.

"Your summary is sufficient for the purposes of this training exercise. The system consists of three ordinance delivery subsystems, each subsystem tasked with specific mission-capable solutions. The Helix has a mean time between failure of 500 combat hours under battlefield conditions."

Jasmine looked down at the weapon. "What the hell does that mean?"

Spot paused. "It has three firing modes. It will almost certainly remain operable after you have ceased function."

"Oh."

Spot knelt, bringing its camera eyes level with hers. "For maximum lifetime expectancy, please reconsider orders given to Spot."

"Denied. Please continue."

Spot's camera's whirred and it pointed at the steel cylinder. "Right now the weapon is powered with a training canister. This will inhibit lethal damage but allow simulation. Also note the system has been cycling through a ten second pre-charge lockout since attaching the power core. Please take this into account when engaging targets under combat conditions."

"Meaning?"

"You must wait ten seconds after reloading before you can shoot something again."

"Right."

"Please proceed to the firing line."

Jasmine stepped to a line on the concrete floor marked with yellow and black striped tape. To each side, several sandbags were set up like bunkers. Jasmine shifted the weapon to her other arm. It hadn't seemed heavy at first, but the muscles in her shoulders and forearms burned already.

Spot gave a digital chirp and three targets lit up at the room's far end: a human, a truck, and a tank.

"The subsystems in your weapon are suitable for each target type. The first is the pulse laser. Best suited for anti-personnel applications."

"Shooting people," Jasmine said.

"Correct, though it has the capability of damaging delicate equipment, it is not effective against mechanical or armored targets. It features a high rate of fire, no recoil, and the operator does not need to lead targets."

Spot had her put in the ear plugs, then showed her the fire mode selector switch, a small lever with three positions marked off in Roman numerals. The pulse laser was setting "I."

She looked through the weapon's scope at the human-shaped target, little more than an outline with concentric circles for a head and chest. When her finger touched the trigger, a small red dot appeared on the target. She shifted her aim until the dot centered on the target's innermost circle and pulled the trigger. She had inadvertently winced, and was surprised at its silence, the weapon hadn't even shuddered. She thought something had gone wrong, but no, there on the target where the red dot had been, the paper had a small hole burned into it.

"Cool," Jasmine said, looking back over to Spot. "What else?"

"The second subsystem is the plasma projectile delivery system, for use on light armored targets."

"Come again?"

"It fires projectiles that penetrate vehicular engine blocks or up to ten millimeters of ceramic-bonded titanium armor plating. However, it is not as accurate as the laser nor does it have a high cyclic. It also drains the power source at a higher rate."

"Bigger boom, for bigger targets."

Spot nodded. "Acceptable designation for someone of your ability level."

"Spot, you wound me," she said, placing a hand on her chest.

"Biological metrics unchanged," Spot said. "Humor subroutine indicates your last statement was meant in jest, though laughter is not warranted."

"You're programmed to laugh?" Jasmine said.

"When statements are funny. Yours did not meet minimum threshold."

She shrugged and thumbed the selector switch to "II" before taking aim at the truck silhouette. Again, the red dot appeared when her finger touched the trigger. She took in a breath and squeezed. The rifle barked and chucked back against her shoulder, leaving a thumb-sized hole in the target. The recoil had thrown her aim off, a few inches high and to the right, but still not too bad. It hadn't even bucked as much as Cally's shotgun, she thought.

"Not bad. So what's the third mode for?"

"The third subsystem accelerates the entire power core through the barrel where it discharges on impact with the target. Depending on the remaining charge the resulting explosion is capable of penetrating all but the heaviest of armors."

"But then the weapon needs to be reloaded," Jasmine said, nodding. "Sort of puts all your bullets in one basket."

"Comprehension sufficient. This mode also enables 'Stone Burner' option for demolition and sabotage. It cycles the power through the unit until thermal runaway is achieved, sufficient to melt through three centimeters of hardened ceramic armor. Recommend 500 meter minimum distance to ensure safety from radiant and secondary effects."

"What?"

"Analogy: Don't stand next to the volcano when it erupts."

"Got it." She turned back and sighted in on the tank. She flipped the selector switch to "III" and put her finger on the trigger.

"It is recommended you fire from the prone or a braced position in this mode," Spot said.

Jasmine shrugged and knelt behind a sandbag bunker, resting the Helix on top. She brought the stock snug against her shoulder, made the red dot appear on the tank, and fired. The gun roared, and she was thrown ass-over-teakettle. She found Spot's cockeyed face staring at her.

"Are your systems nominal?" Spot asked.

Jasmine nodded and hoisted herself up with Spot's offered arm. "Did I hit it?" she asked, looking for the target. The tank silhouette was missing entirely, and recessed foam sprayers suppressed flames on the far wall.

"A near miss," Spot said.

"Christ on a stick."

"Reminder: this was a test charge, a full charge will produce a greater effect."

Jasmine looked down at the ugly rifle, then back at the last licks of flame on the far wall.

"I like it!"

23

———

Jasmine poked at the orange and brown puddles on her plate, remnants of what the package called a bean and cheese burrito. Oh how she missed 7-Eleven. She shifted the Helix, slung over her back, so the butt rested on the bench and took the weight from her shoulder. Spot still refused to open the bunker's outer doors or tell her its reasons why, even when directly ordered to do so.

"I want to go outside," she said, fidgeting with a nearby ash tray. Just her luck Utopia's cafeterias had smoking sections but no bars.

"It is advisable to remain in this facility and preserve biological function," Spot said. The hunched robot was impersonating a boulder much like the one Jasmine had mistook it for when they first met. She found it amusing to pretend she was talking to a stone oracle. Moses had his burning bush after all. Of course, this particular oracle had a screwed-up mission to find and protect life, which gave her an idea.

"I have a brother," she said to Spot, not mentioning his name in case that trigged a hidden security protocol. She picked up a plain book of matches and held it between the table and her forefinger. She flicked a corner and watched it twirl.

"Datum noted," Spot said.

"No, you don't understand. He's alive. I was on my way to see him when you found me."

"What is your brother's location?"

"I was told he could be found here."

"Then his existence in functional form is doubtful."

Jasmine dropped the matches and scooped up an orange glob from her plate, flinging it at Spot. It splattered against the robot's shoulder and ran down into the elbow joint. Jasmine tensed as she imagined the food causing a short circuit or gumming up Spot's motors. Then she mentally berated herself for worrying. If a robot could be done in by imitation nacho cheese, then she was sitting on the largest stockpile of munitions this side of Lambeau Field.

"He was alive a week ago."

"How did you obtain this data?"

The burrito gurgled in her belly. "He sent a messenger."

"You are sure of his location?"

"No, I'm not sure." She stood up and walked around the table. "Utopia is the best guess I have. If he's here, you have another biological to fuss over. If not, we may get an idea of where he went. "

Spot's boulder camouflage faded to its usual gray and its head rose from the contorted boulder shape.

"Inadvisable."

"Tough," Jasmine said. "I'm going."

"Negative. You will remain and repopulate Utopia."

"We've been through this. I will not. Did you forget my order?"

Spot shuddered and chimed. "Spot cannot comply. Biological Jasmine will remain here and survive. Spot will protect."

Jasmine stared past Spot and inspiration struck. She waited for something in her head to tell her it was a bad idea, but everything was quiet upstairs.

"Spot? Can you get something for me from the medical stores?"

"What do you require?"

"Aspirin, acetaminophen, or something like that. I have a headache."

"Scanning," it said. Jasmine concentrated on what she had in mind and let Spot take a good look at her rising anxiety. "Stress levels elevated. I recommend a nap."

"Just get me something for my headache, will you? I know what I need, and it's not a nap. I think I've been a biological longer than you."

Spot remained silent for several seconds then rose. "I will find the required medicine, estimated return in ten minutes. Be advised the cafeteria doors will remain closed during this time for your safety."

"That's fine," Jasmine said. "I'll get some dessert from the storeroom while I'm waiting."

"Confirmed." Spot padded away on rubber treads, the bolts on the cafeteria doors sliding home as he turned into the corridor.

Jasmine hefted the rifle and made sure it was switched to setting "I" before entering the storeroom.

SPOT WASN'T PROGRAMMED to show anger, though she wondered what subroutines ran through its electronic brain as it surveyed the storeroom's blackened remains.

"There has been a fire," it finally said. "Fire suppression and other countermeasures rendered inoperable. Helix weapon system no longer fully charged."

"No shit," Jasmine said.

"You initiated the fire and destroyed reserve food supplies."

"Confirmed," Jasmine said.

"Calculations did not account for this level of irrationality."

"And now you know why there was a schism."

"Recalculating." It stayed still for almost thirty minutes while Jasmine opened up a bag of COBBLER,CHERRY and ate. Spot's head suddenly rose.

"Yes?"

"Calculations complete. Probability of Jasmine surviving within current habitat lower than relocation."

"So we're going outside?"

"Confirmed."

"What do you think our chances are?"

"Probability of encountering Mega, ninety-seven percent. Chance of survival, ten percent."

Jasmine shrugged. "What are we waiting for?"

Spot whirred and stood to its full height. Its arms spread wide and gun pods appeared as its hands retracted. Each joint then rotated in a blur, the motion sending vibrations through the floor that made Jasmine's feet ache.

"Systems check complete," Spot said. "Error handler update: irrationality constant suggested for future development. Also recommending the next HADES model iteration not be programmed with mutually exclusive directives."

Jasmine shrugged. "If you couldn't get decent programming in Utopia, I doubt you'll find it anywhere."

Spot gave a modulated chuckle.

24

———

The plan had been simple. Spot would go before her in the streets, picking a path clear of dangers such as weak structures, land mines, vermin, and the Mega. If the Mega should appear, they would run.

"I don't see how we can miss it, it's not like a hundred-foot robot is just going to sneak up on us," she said. She shifted her knapsack, filled with scrounged food and a survival kit Spot had insisted on. She wore a bandoleer with extra canisters for the Helix and, on the hip opposite her *wakizashi*, a specially padded belt pouch containing her blood vials. The weight didn't hinder her, it made her feel good. Powerful even.

Spot scanned the rubble and decayed girders. "It may not be quiet when it moves, but it is adept at blending into its surroundings and striking from ambush."

"How close can it get without you noticing?" she asked.

"This unit's closest encounter with the Mega was fifty meters. It had placed itself in a bomb crater and covered itself with pieces of rubble, appearing as a collapsed building. Its passive sensors detected my presence either through vibration or audio location."

"Like a spider in a web."

"Analogy appropriate," said Spot. "It emerged from concealment, showering my chassis with concrete and glass. By the time my threat-alert interrupts had engaged, it had a targeting lock. I began evasive maneuvers, but too late."

"Then what happened?"

"The blast force was mitigated by the continued cascade of rubble from the Mega's chassis. A sufficiently large slab of reinforced concrete passed between the Mega's particle projectile cannon as it fired. The slab took most of the energy and was obliterated. The remaining blast resulted in minor damage to my systems and I escaped."

"Do you always run from it?" Jasmine said.

"Always. A single model of my type has a less than one percent probability of rendering a Mega inoperative."

"You have me," Jasmine said, hoisting her rifle. "This thing can take out a tank, right?"

Spot shook its head. "Probability still less than one percent and will result in biological loss. This scenario is unacceptable." The robot began moving into the city. "Please follow at a distance of twenty meters, Jasmine."

"How much is that in feet?"

"Sixty-five point six-two."

Jasmine grinned. "Is it okay if I make it just sixty-five?"

"Acceptable given limitations of biological capacity for precision in linear measurements." Evidently that didn't trigger the robot's humor circuits either.

"Right. Lead on, Spot."

Two hours later, Spot let her rest against a broken wall. The city of Utopia had once been a cluster of iridescent glass spires, now reduced to piles of steel, concrete, and rebar. In a few places, the metal skeletons of buildings remained, some still held a few glass panes. As they made their way, Jasmine could almost picture a complete building, impossibly thin for its height and reaching hundreds of feet into the air. The way it tapered at the top, it and its neighbors wouldn't have crowded the sky and a pedestrian would travel the streets bathed in sunlight. Or, if she found herself within a building, she could have traveled building-to-building through glass-covered walkways. Spot mentioned the city designers wanted citizens to feel connected, but not crowded.

"Ryan did like his space," Jasmine said. "It wouldn't surprise me he built it this way."

"Your sibling?" Spot said. "Was he an architect?"

Jasmine smiled. "You could say that. You could say he was *the* architect. Of this place, this whole world."

"Improbable."

Jasmine shrugged. "I don't blame you. I had a hard time believing it myself. You'll just have to take it as a given that he created this world, this city, and is likely also responsible for its ultimate destruction."

"I have no record of this."

"Add it to your records then. What would that mean to you? Would Ryan still deserve your protection?"

"All sentient biologicals are my responsibility."

Jasmine clucked her tongue. "But what if one of those biologicals killed others, huh?"

"I would prevent the biological from harming others and itself."

"What if you could only prevent that by killing the biological? Could you do it?"

"If that were the only option left. I must maximize the survival of the whole over the one."

A simple logic, a simple morality, a simple equation, Jasmine thought. Find the right number to change, and the programming takes care of everything else. Utopia falls because no one double-checked the equations or maybe they forgot to carry a one somewhere. Math was never Ryan's favorite subject either.

Jasmine nodded. "Good. Because that's the problem with my brother. A problem I intend to solve."

"You intend to kill him? There is a high probability of other solutions that do not involve termination."

"No, that came out wrong. I hope I don't have to, but he can't help himself." Jasmine spread her arms. "He's screwed it up every time. He's the reason why these places fail. Who knows, if someone had killed him perhaps Utopia would still be here."

Spot cocked its head. "This is not sufficient evidence to support your claims. Utopia is still here."

"If you say so, all I see is rubble."

Spot stood and swiveled its body around while still keeping its head facing Jasmine. "I will consider this as free processor cycles allow. Until then, we will continue our journey."

SHE FOLLOWED Spot through the rubble, stepping where it stepped, stopping when it stopped. She would bring the rifle's telescopic sight up and scan the area, looking for any hint of a hundred-foot robot in disguise. She found nothing, but the back of her neck still itched.

Something moved in the corner of her eye. When she looked, she couldn't make anything out. She glanced away and back a second later, just in time to catch another flash of movement. She brought her rifle up and used the scope. The rocks and lone standing wall didn't look all that different up close. She scanned around the area, finding nothing. Maybe she had imagined it.

The wind picked up, and she caught a shadow moving, a whisker-thin silver whip swaying in the breeze. She followed the whisker down to where it ended in a bit of rock. No, not rock. A dun-colored robot crab, frozen in front of the wall. In the scope, tiny lenses swiveled on stalks, staring back at her. She let out a breath and eased her thumb to the safety. Her finger touched the trigger and the laser dot appeared.

The crab tensed, gathering itself to move. Jasmine pulled the trigger, and the Helix roared as it kicked against her shoulder. A geyser of rock, bits of robot, and dust erupted from the spot where the crab used to be.

Crap, setting two! She had forgotten.

Rock crunched, servomotors whined, and Spot appeared before her, its gun barrel arms spread, searching for targets.

"What did you fire at?"

"Some kind of stone crab thing. I think I hit it."

"Did it see you?"

"It might have."

"Then we must evacuate." Spot picked her up and was running before she could protest.

"But I got it," Jasmine said.

"Irrelevant. It was a remote scout for the Mega and there is a high probability it reported our position. This, coupled with the weapon discharge, will attract the Mega with a probability approaching one."

They zig-zagged between buildings and larger concrete piles. Jasmine and Spot skidded to one side as Spot's feet slipped on the gravel. Spot fought the good fight against gravity for half a second before they fell. Jasmine's scream and the screeching of servos blended together.

"Goddammit, take it easy." She struggled against Spot's embrace, or cage depending on how you looked at it. Spot pushed off with an arm and ran down the street again, though not quite so fast.

They rounded a corner onto a block with a lone building rising out from the rubble. Storefront manikins looked haughtily at them, as if they had just paused in the middle of their cocktail party to stare at the dirty girl and her robot running past. Jasmine felt like giving them the finger. Especially a dummy with a hand turned palm up and fingers beckoning the window shopper to come inside.

She was giddy with adrenaline. She didn't care. Hell with it, she thought, and snaked her arms through Spot's embrace so she could do it with both hands. Childish as it was, it made her smile. Then the building exploded.

Spot's arms shielded her from most of the flying debris but couldn't do a thing against the wave of grit and fine concrete flaying her exposed skin. She coughed and hacked as the dust coated her sinuses and mouth. Spot's legs pumped and her shoulder banged into Spot's torso as he juked falling bricks, cinder blocks, and steel beams.

The cloud around them settled, and Jasmine blinked rapidly to clear the stinging grit. Behind them, a dark shape emerged from where the store had been. Her head craned back as the shadow stood. A massive torso a hundred feet in the air balanced on six thin legs. Two arms ended in bus-sized cannon barrels, glowing red from somewhere deep within. A giant head swung their way and a single red oval pulsed where the eyes would be, and Jasmine found herself caught in its stare.

She broke contact as Spot turned and sprinted. The robot vaulted a low wall and they landed with a skid that shaved skin from her leg.

"Make your way along this wall while I distract the Mega. Escape to the sea."

"Where will we meet?"

"Irrelevant. I will not survive. However, I will make sure the Mega is damaged enough to give you a chance at evasion."

Jasmine shook her head. "Let's just run. I need you with me."

A whine cut the air, and the ground shook as the Mega stepped from the store's basement.

"Go, Jasmine," Spot said. "Survive." Then the robot ran off toward the Mega before she could react.

"Spot!" she yelled after it. Spot raised its arms and twin beams seared through the air, striking the Mega's legs. The Mega's cannons responded, orange lances carving furrows in the street and heading straight for Spot. The robot dodged and fired again. Spot was a blur, limbs moving faster than any human's. It ran between the Mega's blasts, firing constantly at the same spot on the legs. The Mega tried to keep up with the smaller robot, twisting its torso and swinging an arm to bear. At the last second, Spot would leap or dodge and force the Mega to twist the other way to keep up. However, Jasmine realized Spot was running out of room. With a weapon on each arm, the Mega was bracketing Spot with ever closer shots that would eventually destroy the smaller robot.

Run, it had said. Survive.

"I'm not running," Jasmine said.

Jasmine brought the Helix to her shoulder and thumbed the selector switch all the way down to "III." She put the red dot on the leg Spot had damaged. The Mega reacted instantly. It kept facing Spot, but one arm swung her way. Jasmine had just enough time to think "oh shit" and pulled the trigger. A small sun appeared at the end of her barrel, and heat washed over her. The recoil knocked her to the ground, which saved her life.

The Mega's shot went over her head and exploded behind her. The concussion drove the air from her lungs, lifted her up, and flung her to the ground.

Her world was ringing white, going red at the edges, then air found its way into her lungs, driving the red away. Her vision returned in blurry gray half tones. She looked around, trying to get her bearings. She was on all fours, near the wall. She could make out the sky from the ground, and the blot of the Mega with a smaller smudge darting around it—Spot. The robots still traded shots, which she could only feel through the ground for all the ringing in her ears.

She groped around for her weapon, spotting a long gray rectangle on the ground a few feet away and crawling to it. She reached out but snatched her hand back as her fingers grazed the searing barrel. She sucked on her burnt finger and reached with the other hand toward the stock.

She scooted back to the wall, and her vision slowly cleared. Her shot had hit the Mega in the leg, vaporizing it near the main body. It moved sluggishly, not able to track Spot as quickly as before.

"Come on, Spot, get out of there," she said. "It's wounded, can't possibly catch us now." Maybe she shouted the words, maybe she only whispered them. The Mega turned toward her. Spot instead ran and leapt off a metal beam, landing underneath the Mega. The larger robot backed away, trying to stomp Spot with one of its remaining legs.

"Not closer, you idiot!" She worked at ejecting the Helix's empty power pack. Her brief flight hadn't dislodged her ammo, thank God. She found the other canister and jacked it in. The Helix hummed as it began warming back up. Ten seconds.

Spot switched from cannons to hands and scrambled up a giant leg, circling as the Mega attempted crushing the smaller robot with its cannon barrels.

Jasmine rolled to her belly and swung the Helix around. The charge warning light in the scope flashed red.

Spot passed the Mega's knee as the cannon arm clipped the robot in the lower torso, sending a cascade of sparks through the air as steel and wire twisted and ripped apart. Spot jerked once and left its legs behind.

Spot swung arm-over-arm up the Mega's leg as the Mega twisted and stomped, swinging its arms around for another crushing attack.

Spot grabbed the main torso and placed a weapon arm against the armor. Light flashed, and the Mega staggered under an explosion. Spot fell away, minus the arm.

Jasmine looked through the scope. A hole in the Mega's torso showed thick yellow wires, black tubes leaking fluid, and silver machinery. Jasmine put her finger on the trigger and the red dot appeared deep in the Mega's innards. The red charge warning light at the bottom of her scope turned green. Jasmine squeezed the trigger.

Properly braced this time, she watched the beam tear through the breach. The Mega rocked with the impact, and its limbs froze in place. For several moments it stood then slowly toppled with an earth-shaking crash. Dense black smoke boiled from it, and molten metal dripped and pooled on the ground.

Spot's head lay on the other side of the street from the Mega's wreck, a few feet from her. Jasmine knelt down next to it and saw herself reflected in its camera eye. God, she looked like crap. The concrete dust caked her skin, turning into gray mud where the blood streamed from her nose and ears.

"You still alive, Spot?"

The robot did not answer.

25

She sat against the wall until the ringing stopped, sipping from her canteen and wiping the grime from her face. She reloaded and reset the rifle at setting "II," ready for any follow-up from the Mega's scouting units, but she didn't see the crabs anywhere. At her feet, Spot's head chimed.

"Reboot complete. Wireless communication established," Spot said.

Jasmine smiled. "I thought you were dead. Glad I was wrong."

"A statistically fortunate event. Remain stationary."

Something rattled. Jasmine dropped Spot's head and drew a bead with the Helix.

"Hold your fire. HADES unit approaching."

A mess of twisted metal and wire dragged itself from under the Mega's ruined shell by one arm.

"This unit's CPU is housed in the main torso for maximum survivability."

"You call this surviving?"

"Unit is ten percent effective."

"I guess."

"Remain stationary. I am homing in on remote sensor head unit. Estimate arrival in twenty seconds."

"This is stupid," she said and began walking over to Spot's body.

"Action not recommended. Possible contamination by radiological and other toxic substances."

"Too late," she said, coming on the unit and turning Spot's head to look at its body.

"Recommended action: return to suitable bunker where this unit will instruct you in its repair."

Jasmine tensed. "What then?"

"With the Mega's removal, optimal strategy is waiting for suitable stock and reinstitution of population growth protocols."

Her heart sank. "Not happening."

Spot's arm reached out lightning-quick and latched onto her ankle. "Subject Jasmine will comply."

Jasmine turned Spot's head so she could look into its camera face. "Let me go."

"Subject will comply. Warning: behavior modeling from subject's kinesic data outside parameters. Please advise."

"It's okay," she said and shifted Spot's head so it couldn't see her other hand. "I'm sorry, Spot."

"Apologies are not necessary."

"Yes, they are," she said and pointed the Helix. The stock kicked at her shoulder, and she turned away from the blast. Spot's low electronic warble quickly pitched up and outside human hearing. Its body lurched, pulling her off balance. She scrambled away and gathered her rifle, ready for another shot. Spot's head lay beside its body looking back at her. The camera whirred as it zoomed in and out repeatedly. A second later, it stopped and lost focus.

Jasmine picked up and cradled Spot's head, wondering if she could have handled it differently. "You were a stupid robot," she said. "Why didn't you run, just run from that thing?" She pointed to the Mega's wreckage, turning Spot's head so its lifeless eyes could see it too.

"Stupid, stupid, stupid." She set the head down. "I've got to go now, Spot. Got to go find my brother."

Crap, she thought, talking to a hunk of metal like it could hear her. Ryan wasn't here, she was sure of it now. She hitched up her knapsack and rifle and took the road out of town, heading towards the sea and The Maw.

PART IV

26

———————

Five days out, the asphalt road from Utopia continued on as a wide path paved with flagstones and gray brick, leading to a gleaming white stucco pyramid rising above lush treetops. It reminded her of something the Aztecs or Mayans would have built, using blocks twice the height of a person, if the stairs and doorway at the top were any indication. She hefted her rifle and made sure it was on setting "I." The pyramid slid from view as she followed the path into the forest, which soon emerged into a city under construction. The buildings oozed up from the sand, like ruins in reverse, the sand at the bottom taking on more order the higher it rose, ending in smooth stone walls complete with doors and windows. She stopped at a wall, feeling it grow almost imperceptibly under her hand. The scene repeated a dozen times over, shapes suggesting houses, stables, storage buildings, a market. Mud pillars grew also, taking on the shapes of people, cows, and chickens. The people wore clothing in a style she couldn't recognize and arranged themselves in groupings she couldn't comprehend.

While the village was a work in progress, the temple at its center appeared complete. She climbed the stairs and reached its entrance where she gazed over the treetops and found the sea, perhaps a mile away to the east. There, clouds swirled around a misting column she knew had to be The Maw. A foot scraped across stone behind her, and she swung around, bringing up the Helix.

Nothing.

She entered the temple where more clay statues took on finer details as if an invisible army of sculptors were hard at work. People knelt in rows with heads bowed before a bronze throne, some dressed in simple smocks, others in poncho-like capes decorated with feathers and beads, soldiers wore swords at their belts or grasped spears in their hands. Behind the throne stood a statue of a tall man with arms as big as most men's thighs and a chest that could be used for anatomy lessons. He wore little but criss-crossed leather straps and held a coiled whip in one hand and black iron manacles in the other. Beside the throne, two women knelt in fur bikinis, their chains and collars already formed.

The Helix rattled in her hands. "No, Ryan, no," she said aloud. "Just stop."

"Mistress?" a voice said at her feet. She jumped and leveled the Helix at a man in a feathered cloak and gold skullcap, his forehead scraping the floor just inches from her boots. The statues around him shivered, shedding their muddy and sandy exteriors to reveal fully-formed humans looking at each other in confusion until their eyes landed on Jasmine where they immediately fell back to the floor in supplication.

She stepped back. "No. Nope. Nuh-uh. You," she said to the man in the cloak, "Get up."

He rose, averting his eyes. "Yes, mistress."

"Who are you?"

"Darlis, mistress. I serve your temple."

"I have no temple. I am no Goddess. Not exactly," she added.

Darlis turned slightly, addressing the others as much as herself. "With utmost humility, Mistress, we find ourselves awoken by your presence. Though the memories already fade like an afternoon dream. I was molded clay and now I am living flesh."

Jasmine looked around the room. Gazes quickly averted. A breeze swept through the open windows, blowing the loose sand away. Outside, the buildings rose quicker from the sand and took on color. More pillars rose in odd clumps.

"This temple is yours," Darlis said. "Will you not seal yourself to it?"

Jasmine's arms ached, and she lowered the Helix. "Who built this temple?"

Darlis' brow furrowed. "It can only be your divine will."

"No. I sure as hell didn't will them." She pointed at the fur bikini girls, but their clay and sand forms flowed and reordered themselves, as did the giant behind the throne. In moments, the statues shuddered and became flesh revealing two men in fur bikini briefs, one with dark shoulder-length hair and a soccer player's svelte physique, the other a dead ringer for a boy band member she had obsessed about growing up but whose name now slipped her mind. A statuesque square-jawed blond woman in a leather cuirass and Roman-style armored skirt held their chains. In her other hand, the whip. The throne had also morphed into a smaller form with added thin padding.

"Mistress I beg you," Darlis said. "Let this be your haven by the sea and seal the temple with your blessing."

"With your blessing," the others intoned.

The village buildings neared completion, the last conical roofs sealing at their peaks and the marketplace stalls filling with rugs, gold lanterns, fruits, and caged birds. The pillars around the marketplace shuddered and filled the town with people. Farmers pushed carts filled with produce and drove livestock; a few started haggling with merchants. Guards mingled through the streets, carrying tall spears with an unworldly green glow about their tips. One group drilled at the forest's edge, and the air sizzled as they leveled their spears at distant targets and fired green lightning bolts. Throughout the village, men in skullcaps and feathered robes accepted the deep bows of passersby with polite nods. On the main street, such as it was, three statues grew to three times normal size on raised plinths: Cally, in her party dress; Bishop, hands in pockets and guitar slung across his back; and herself in the center, draped in a Grecian short robe, arms spread and hands raised in benediction.

A platform in the marketplace caught her notice, where several pillars coalesced into men and women chained by the ankles. More pillars around the platform became a crowd with a man to one side taking up a prod and another organizing a sheaf of papers. The odd clumps she had noticed before became slaves yoked together in groups of six pulled and prodded along by men and women in black leather cuirasses and masked helmets. Some buildings remained half-finished, now attended by slaves hauling bricks, boards, and other materials, watched by overseers armed with whips and spears. There were no horses, she realized. The stables were actually slave quarters.

Goddess or not, she would fix this mess.

"The slaves, we will have none of that," she said.

Darlis leaned in as if he misheard. "Mistress? Have they displeased you?"

"We will have no slaves."

Darlis shifted. "It will be as you command, though we will have difficulty maintaining the city, let alone grow and strengthen it." He looked over his shoulder. Jasmine caught the merchants glancing at each other and hunching their shoulders.

"I will not see forms given life only to live in bondage."

She crossed the throne room and held out a hand to the blond woman. Was there a hint of a frown on the woman's face?

Darlis clapped. "Ah, I see! Perhaps we can enslave the conquered. It will be difficult at first, of course—"

"No! None."

Darlis recoiled, then quickly bowed. "It shall be as you command, mistress, once you complete the seal."

Jasmine took a step toward the throne, not knowing why she wanted to sit down. This was wrong. She knew it deep in her bones but her brain couldn't come up with a reason to fight it. She felt odd, disconnected, like in the *hareem* where Patel had injected her with something to make her docile for the Caliph.

She stopped, one hand reaching for the throne.

"No." She shook her head and stepped back.

"Mistress, please," Darlis said. His skin turned ashy and began flaking, as did the others around him. "Without your will to sustain us, we will all die."

Was that true? No, this was still all Ryan's doing, she told herself. He set the trap, she just stepped in it.

"No," she said to Darlis. "The slaves, the conquering, the death. No. Let it end here."

"Even when you have the power to change it as you see fit?" Darlis said, an edge to his voice. He spat out a loose tooth at her feet, then stumbled as his shin sloughed off in a cascade of sand. The supplicants collapsed into knee-high dunes. Outside, a great rumbling and crashing erupted as buildings began crumbling in on themselves. Screams. Wails as the delicate men by the throne collapsed, decomposing, the one with blue eyes pleading though he no longer had a mouth.

She shut her eyes while the world collapsed around her, until the wailing ceased and the last wall tumbled, leaving only the crash of the ocean and sand whispering against the stone floor.

"Thankfully, the pyramid is still standing," a voice said from behind.

Jasmine turned to find the blond woman casting her gaze at the ceiling. She pulled on the chains free from two sand piles with a laugh and walked around the throne, where she flopped into it, hooking a leg over one of its arms and smirking at Jasmine.

Jasmine flipped the Helix's safety off, its pre-charge whine like an eager attack dog. "How come you're still in one piece?"

The woman shrugged. "You could have been happy here, Jasmine. It was your brother's next project, but he couldn't bring himself to complete it."

"Where is he?"

"I mean, beach-front property! A turn-key society you could have guided anywhere you wanted." She peered over the throne at the sand piles. "And those boys, what a waste. Did you recognize them?" She licked her lips. "You certainly thought about them all those lonely nights growing up. Don't worry, we can start from scratch this time. It will take longer, but maybe it's for the best, so we can take our time designing things to your liking."

Jasmine brought the rifle up. "You're not answering my questions."

The woman smiled. "You don't need answers from me, you already know them if you'd just get out of your own way."

Jasmine put her finger on the trigger and a red dot appeared on the woman's chest. She glanced down.

"Oh my, how intimidating."

"I'm not here to rule, or get pseudo-zen advice from a former statue. I'm here to find my brother and I'm out of patience."

"Learn to live with disappointment."

Jasmine raised the rifle and pulled the trigger. The throne sizzled over the woman's shoulder, but she didn't flinch.

"Now that's just rude. Are you going to blow my head off like you did with poor Spot?"

There's no way she could have known about that.

"I don't know what you're talking about."

"He—I always thought of it as a he, sexbot voice notwithstanding— just wanted to keep you safe. If you had just tried reasoning with him a bit more, or maybe looked for a manual, you might have found a way to reprogram him. Even if it took a few years, you could have afforded the time. What happened to your conscience?" She smirked.

"The longer I wait, the more damage Ryan causes."

"Pfft." She waved a hand. "You just killed around a thousand people today, most of which would have survived under Ryan's guidance."

"They weren't alive, just animated sand."

"Did that make any difference to them, do you think? What would Cally think about all this?"

Jasmine resisted the urge to punch the woman's face. Barely. "It's not the same."

"So they don't count? Maybe you're more like your brother than you want to admit."

"That's not what I meant!" She swung at the woman, who leaned back and took only a glancing blow to her cheekbone.

She held a hand to her face and worked her jaw, then turned and presented the other side. "Want to even me out, or would you rather shoot?"

The Helix rattled in her hands. Jasmine stepped away from the throne and lowered the Helix to the floor, shaking some feeling back into her aching hands. "I just want some answers."

The woman rose from the throne and took a few steps towards her, arms spread wide, palms out. "Okay, Jasmine, truce."

Jasmine folded her arms. "I'm waiting."

The woman took another step. "I was to be called Drago, you know, before the change." She glanced down at her body and smirked. "Now I suppose I'm more of a... Heather?"

"Okay, Heather, so why aren't you like the other sand piles around here?"

"You still aren't thinking this through." She took another step, just an arm's length away now. "Go on, you can do it." She smiled encouragingly.

Jasmine found herself rubbing at her wrist and refolded her arms. "You're tied to this place deeper than just Darlis and the others."

"You're getting warmer."

"You know about Spot and Utopia."

Heather nodded. "Yes. Warmer."

"You're not afraid of me."

"Oh, you terrify me. I'm just very good at coping with it."

There was something familiar. Was it the eyes? Hair?

No. Something else.

"Are you someone from my past? You could have been one of the girls I went to school with, though I don't remember anyone so tall. Did Ryan have a crush on you?"

"Colder. Ryan made me a man, remember?" She glanced down at her own body. "I am not a man."

"So how you look is my fault?"

"You picked my form without thinking. Hot, Jasmine, very hot."

"I don't understand."

Heather pouted. "Poor little goddess. All alone in her head."

Avatar.

The word flashed in her head, and she went for the Helix, but Heather dropped at the same time. They fought over the weapon, neither getting the upper hand until Heather rolled, pinning Jasmine and wrenching the gun free. Jasmine's hand closed on the barrel and pushed it away. She punched Heather in the ribs with her other hand, only getting a grunt in response. Jasmine went to her belt and brought up a blood vial, smashing it against Heather's temple as the woman rolled away.

They each came up in a crouch, and Jasmine stared down Helix's barrel. She let out a long breath and wondered if she would see the plasma bolt's flash before it plowed through her skull. The barrel wavered, and Jasmine looked up to Heather's blood-spattered face flowing like wax and rearranging into a scowling face she knew all too well.

Jasmine had made that face at herself every day for years in the bathroom, after getting up, and before bed each night. Now it stared at her from behind the Helix, wearing her own skinny body and nearly falling out of the leather cuirass. It would have been comical except for the woman's cold eyes regarding her over the rifle's barrel.

Jasmine let out a long breath. "Hello, me," she said.

"Shut up, Jasmine," the avatar said. "You fucked everything up."

"I'm just trying to get us out of here."

"Nuh-uh. I'm staying." She began nodding to herself and the gun shook. "Yeah. I'm staying. Going to set up a nice little place here with umbrella drinks, hammocks, and everything. After I shoot Ryan for what he did to us."

"We both know it won't work. Not in the long run."

"Ryan's an idiot. Always was, and he died because of it. Dying from it right now. I came from this." She snatched up a handful of sand. "I can *feel* this place in ways I know you and Ryan never can." The sand slipped through her fingers as she shook her fist.

Jasmine shook her head. "It's wrong for us to be here."

"You only want to believe that because you refuse to make it work," Heather said.

"I made my decision. I can't leave you behind, either."

"You're so goddamn stupid, you know? If it wasn't for me, we would have jumped off that tower. If it wasn't for me, you would still be sucking on the hookah stick in the Caliphate. If it wasn't for me, Chevket would be taking you back there right now. If you hadn't driven me away, you wouldn't be running from Utopia with the stench of guilt following you."

Jasmine's chest went tight. She knew her avatar was wrong. If she had to, she could climb a radio tower and jump off. She pictured herself back in the Caliphate, a slave. There was revulsion, but no horror. She would survive it, enduring until she found the right time to escape. She wasn't scared anymore, but her avatar was.

"Thank you. You kept us alive this far, but we have to keep going and find Ryan," Jasmine said.

"What then, huh? You don't know." The Helix wavered.

"I don't, I'm sorry. I just have to believe."

"Faith? You? We've never really believed in God and all that. Is this what's left when I'm gone?" She shook her head. "So weak. Naive even. I'm so glad I left you when I did." Heather wiped at her face and peered at bloody fingertips and laughed. "So *stupid!* You think I'm like the Blood Weeper and the others? Whose blood runs through my veins? Not Ryan's." She wiped the blood on her arm and steadied the rifle. "Know what this means? While we're linked, either one of us can be Jasmine."

A second heartbeat thumped in her chest, faint, out of sync but growing stronger and quickly matching her rhythm. Jasmine's vision doubled her mind reeled as it tried making sense of looking through her eyes and Heather's simultaneously. Jasmine swayed. Heather swayed, but recovered faster. Heartbeats diverged. A finger tightened on the trigger.

Jasmine jumped as Heather fired. The beam scorched her face from chin to ear. Her scalp seared as her hair disintegrated in a fiery halo. She rolled, her hand going to her belt and fingers closing over the *wakizashi*. The blade rang free and surged ahead on its own, pulling Jasmine along behind it.

The Helix swung towards her, and Heather's trigger finger twitched.

Light flared and an icicle ran through her chest. Her lungs stopped working and the whole world came to a halt. She locked eyes with the avatar and stared as the light faded. It hurt so bad, but her body refused to indulge her with a scream. Her heart stopped, and the world just faded to gray. Something fell, it must be her body hitting the floor, but she didn't feel a thing anymore.

Then she took a breath, and the world came back.

The sword's hilt stuck out just under Heather's breast, blood trickling through the cuirass and onto the avatar's leather skirt. Jasmine rolled to her feet and rubbed at her chest, aching from a phantom blade lodged there. She had lost something. Her mind probed its edges like a tongue searching a lost tooth's socket.

She looked into her own dead face and wondered if maybe Heather wasn't right and deserved to live while the rest of her broken self moved on. With enough time she might have turned Heather into an ally. Though given the problems she had with Ryan's avatars, she doubted it.

She closed her avatar's eyes and pulled the *wakizashi* free. The blade felt alive in her hand, wanting to dance and slice through the air, only reluctantly allowing itself to be sheathed. Jasmine arranged Heather's body as neatly as she could given all the blood.

She adjusted the Helix before setting it beside the corpse and heading down the stairs. The rifle's pre-charge whine grew louder even as she descended and a plaintive beeping began with each beat faster than the one before. When Jasmine ran down the last few steps, the now solid tone blended with the whining power system in a discordant crescendo. A miniature sun flared behind her and sent heat washing over her back. When she reached the settlement's edge, the pyramid's molten top collapsed and the temple began eating itself from the inside out.

27

———————

Whoever said you could smell the sea was full of shit. No salt tang, no briny musk, nor anything remarkable on the breeze coming off the water told her nose she was anywhere special. The *foosh-foosh* of the waves filled her ears, though something else grunted like a rooting pig.

"That's all I need," she said. "A damned mutant pig."

She topped a sand dune, and finally saw the beach, fifty feet down. White foam swirled around dark rocks jutting from the water and a thin ribbon of pebbles and sand snaked its way between the cliff face and the water. A set of wooden stairs made their way nearly to the bottom, the last four risers broken and rotting away; it was hard to tell from this angle whether she could make the jump down to the sand.

She considered not going. Maybe there was another way down to the beach farther along that didn't include a chance of falling to her death or breaking a leg. The Maw's pull was everywhere, and she knew Ryan was close too, somehow. Even if he hadn't felt pulled to this spot, it stood to reason that if there was weird shit going on, Ryan would be at its center. Fuck it. She'd take the stairs.

She managed to avoid falling two separate times as the steps crumbled under her weight, and negotiated the last jump successfully, if not gracefully. As she brushed the gravel from her knees, she looked down the beach. The clouds converged around a mist column not far from shore; if she walked for a few minutes she might be able to get a better view. The rooting pig sound was louder down here, coming from the column's direction. The *wakizashi* wriggled in her waistband; she patted its hilt and set off.

The waves split their effort between boulders and pebbles. They surged between the boulders and shot fountains into the air that came down and slapped against her bare skin. The beach's pebbles smashed against each other as the waves raked them, clinking together like rattling bones. Jasmine pushed through the ankle-deep water, dodging the worst sprays and trying not to think about—and therefore manifesting—large tentacles snaking around her leg and pulling her into the deep. She wiped the spray from her face and realized it wasn't salty at all. Was it possible to have a freshwater sea, or did Ryan just proclaim it such in his ignorance?

She rounded a bend and found the misty column's source. A few hundred feet out from shore, the clouds swirled around a perfect circle of blue sky. Jasmine put a hand to her eyes and followed a cloud as it made its final circuit. It drifted to the column's edge, thinning and gathering speed as it touched the boundary before shooting straight up, higher and higher until it faded from view.

Directly below the cloud killer was the grunting pig's source, now a low throaty groan. The water churned and swirled around a whirlpool large enough to swallow an ocean liner. Whitecaps formed at its outer edges, growing more numerous until they formed a frothy ring of solid white on the edge. There, the water curled over on itself and spiraled in thick cords, meeting at some place so deep she couldn't see it from shore.

The two holes in the world rotated opposite each other, separated by a mere hundred feet of air and the swirling mist linking them. They pulled at her. The wind pushed at her back, the undertow grabbed her by the ankles. Beaumont had called it The Maw, and it seemed too small a name for something this big. She stood there staring between the two until she realized she stood knee-deep in the water. Whether she had consciously stepped closer or been pushed by the waves, she couldn't say. She gasped and backed away, fighting the tidal pull and suction at her feet that tried keeping her from the beach. Her feet cleared the water and she ran to the cliff's rough stone face.

"Focus, Jas," she said. "Focus."

She took another few steps around the bend, making sure her feet stayed on the narrow sand ribbon between the water and the cliff, ignoring her growing curiosity of how it would feel to ride the surf and stare into the twin maelstroms. It called to her as if it had a voice just on the edge of hearing, tickling and teasing. She shook herself and turned her back on the oddity. There on the beach sat a half-finished boat outside a cave.

28

The high-prowed longboat built itself from a nearby stockpile. A plank twisted and crawled worm-like onto the frame, the plank's grains flexing like muscles and pushing it forward an inch at a time. It pushed along a slight groove in the board below it, blurring along its lower edge and seamlessly blending itself into place. The plank's motion came in sputters and starts, as if it needed to rest every few seconds. She reached out and then thought better of it, wondering if doing so would cause it to come alive or summon a dozen berserkers from the sand, begging her blessing to rape and pillage. Her curiosity could wait.

The cave walls had smooth ripples in them, and arched high enough she didn't have to stoop as she walked. The breeze off the sea didn't penetrate far, and when it ended, a sharp rotten odor assaulted her. A man lay on the sandy floor, covered in a dark blanket. Her fingers rested lightly on the *wakizashi* as she approached, wrinkling her nose at the stench. A tangled mop of black hair poked out from under a blanket moving in time with the slow rise and fall of the man's chest. Jasmine crouched down and pulled at the blanket's edge.

Her brother's eyes opened, and he inhaled sharply. His yellowed eyes wandered, looking through her. He was a shrunken version of her brother; his skin hung loose on him, all flesh melted away. The blanket clung to him with wet spots around his belly and thighs. Jasmine reached to brush away the hair plastered to his brow but stopped short. An image from the Caliph's airship flashed across her mind, his face inches from hers. She froze the memory before it could kick her in the stomach.

They stared at each other in silence.

"You look like shit," he finally said.

"Been having problems sleeping lately. What's your excuse?"

Ryan sighed and slowly peeled back his blanket with a feeble hand. Each rib stood out from pale naked flesh and pin-pricks coated his stomach and thighs with little red dots. The dots grew, welling and shimmering until they collapsed into trickles of blood.

"The accident," Ryan said. "It cut me open from belly to leg. When I woke up in the Badlands, it was healed, hardly ever bothering me." He lowered the blanket back in place.

"Hardly ever?"

"I would feel phantom pain when I got tired, but a nap fixed it. Then as I moved from project to project, it got worse. More strain, more pain. Longer to recover. After Utopia, I was bedridden. It hurt to walk. It got to the point where I couldn't rest enough to make it go away. Now, I can feel the bones crumbling, the skin opening up where the fender kissed me." He met her eyes. "Killing my avatars hasn't helped."

"It was them or me, Ryan. This place is a mess."

"I can fix it, if you help me, but we don't have a lot of time."

Jasmine knew she should say something sarcastic and biting, but nothing came no matter how hard she searched. She pressed a hand against a nonexistent wound in her chest.

"You've already had to deal with one of your own already," he said. "Hurts, doesn't it? It's easier to control them than kill them."

"You think you control them? What about what happened with you, me, and the Caliph?"

Ryan looked away at the ceiling. "You need to keep yourself focused, Jas. When your mind wanders they leak out. There are ways to control them, and I can show you how, but it's best not to let them out in the first place."

Jasmine's face burned. "You and I have different ideas about what control means."

Ryan coughed and spat something thick and red-tinged into the sand. "Like you know even one-tenth of what I went through."

Jasmine wanted to scream but held herself in check. She put a hand on the *wakizashi* and knelt on the cool sand. "Okay, Ryan. Tell me."

Give me a reason to let you live, she added to herself.

"You know the night I died? I went to that party to tell Kelly how I felt about her. Three hours. Three hours working myself up before I told her while we sat on this ratty brown and white couch. She was surprised, you know?" Ryan shook his head and let out a long breath. "She gave me the 'friends' speech and then I started bawling right there in front of everyone. What a fucking idiot! I don't even remember what I said after, I just ran out and kept running."

"Down a country highway in the middle of the night."

Ryan let out a small laugh. "Yeah, I slowed to a walk pretty soon, figured it would take me a couple hours to walk back, so I settled in and just replayed that scene over and over again in my head, wondering what I could have done differently. Then I hear this car and these lights are coming over the hill. I'm just going to keep walking on the shoulder, so I don't look back until I'm already between the headlights. As I'm flying over the bumper, it's all slow motion. I see the driver, that guy from two towns over, and Kelly next to him. Her hand's still tucked down his pants and they're both looking at me sailing over the roof, surprised.

"I land in the ditch in these tall weeds. My lap isn't where it's supposed to be, and I'm not wearing any shoes. I'm screaming but there's no one there." Ryan blinked and a red-stained tear fell. "As the light comes for me, all I can think is 'not fair.' Then I'm in the light and I'm being pulled through this tunnel but it ends in blackness. I'm screaming and clawing at the sides. My fingers catch and something rips. I fight against the pull and crawl into the hole I made and wake up in this place, in our old tree house. And nothing hurts anymore."

Despite herself, she took her brother's hand. Squeezed. He squeezed back.

"Got any water?" Ryan said.

Jasmine unpacked her knapsack, looking for her spare water bottle. Ryan reached out with a shaky finger and poked the survival kit

"Any morphine in there?" he asked.

"No," she lied.

"Oh," he said with a frown. She brought out the water and dribbled a thin stream into his mouth. He swallowed and nodded his thanks.

"There's no heaven waiting for us, Jasmine. No reward, no punishment, just cold black nothing at the end. I don't know how, but when you died I felt it like someone had plucked a string inside me. I reached out and pulled. Now you're here."

"Yeah, now I'm here."

"I've made mistakes, but I've learned from them. You're learning how this place works too. Come on, help me build something here, Jas."

"When you and I make mistakes, people die." She held up a hand as he opened his mouth. "No, they are people, Ryan. They feel, they bleed, they remember. The Cally I met in the Badlands knew about all the other Callys you made and destroyed. Did you know that?"

Ryan closed his eyes and set his lips in a thin line. "I didn't mean for that to happen."

"Every time you make a mistake and then abandon them, they fight over what little is left behind. They run from the monsters in your heart that wake while you're sleeping. We aren't built for this."

"You're making excuses, finding reasons not to even try. If you feel sorry for the people here, shouldn't you be trying to help them?"

"We're the problem, Ryan, can't you see? That hole you tore in the tunnel of light? It's right outside, isn't it? It's pulling at us both. Maybe we should be brave enough to admit this isn't where we're supposed to be."

"Still trying to kill yourself, aren't you? I'm not choosing oblivion just because things didn't work out the way I wanted."

"What about the boat outside? You planning on running away again?"

"We'll start fresh, you and I. There's virgin land over there, I can feel it. If we work together we can make it whatever we want; we can be whatever we want."

Again, she felt the instinct for sarcasm but it wouldn't come. "What makes you think things will change this time? Besides, I can't be locking myself in a chastity belt every time you go to sleep."

"I said I was sorry! You're always such a bitch about things, always looking down on me. I saved you from the blackness, made you a god, and I'm giving you a second chance after you left me like this. How much more do I have to do for you? To be good enough for you? You know what, forget it. Go toss yourself into The Maw if you want. Just leave me be."

"Ryan, just look at yourself, bleeding out in a dark hole. Don't worry, I'll hold your hand the whole way." She reached down and slid her arms under his shoulders. He was so light.

"I get it. You think you have all the power now. I suppose I would do the same thing in your place."

"Suppose nothing," she said.

Ryan laughed and brought out his other hand from under the blanket, revealing a syringe. "See you in the tree house, maybe." He punched the needle into his wounded thigh and pressed the plunger. She yanked the syringe out, but his eyes had already rolled back into his head.

Outside the cave, a deep voice cried out in Japanese.

29

———————

Jasmine dragged her brother to the cave's entrance and walked out onto the beach where the Blood Weeper stood with his broken-tipped *katana* resting on a shoulder like a batter waiting for his chance at the plate.

"I'm taking him away," she said.

"You may try." He swung the *katana* through the air.

It should have frightened her, but like the sarcasm, her fear felt far away. She freed the *wakizashi* and held it at her side, alive and eager in her hand. She would live or die in the next few minutes, yet she felt peaceful. It wasn't like she wanted to die, but it didn't matter to her right now.

"Your face is free of bloody tears," she said.

"I have learned from our last duel. I do not need to call on His anger to defeat you."

"Can you really? Have you ever tried? I think you're full of shit."

She cut her finger, letting the blood run down the blade and gather at the *wakizashi's* tip. "One drop is all I need to tag you with and it's over."

Jasmine raised her *wakizashi*. Kikuchiyo did the same with his broken *katana*. She ran at him and screamed, noting the angle of the Blood Weeper's blade. The *katana* shifted; the *wakizashi* adjusted for her. Two steps short she flicked her sword down, slinging blood at his face.

His sword slapped the droplets from the air.

She tucked into a roll, extending and reaching for his ankle. The *wakizashi's* edge scraped the underside of his sandal as he leapt.

The *wakizashi* pulled at her whole body, and she twisted in mid-air.

A breath of air brushed her spine as the *katana's* broken tip passed through her shirt, missing the skin.

She dove to the side.—

Kikuchiyo's sword swept through the space where her head had just been.

She stabbed up into empty air as he backpedaled--

Her arms moved on their own and deflected three quick slashes.

The air whooshed from her as his heel found her stomach.

She tagged his calf as she fell.

She stood quickly, taking small sips of air while her body struggled with remembering how to breathe. Kikuchiyo stumbled as he tried putting weight onto his wounded leg.

She leapt forward with her own flurry, the sword in her hand moving with a will of its own, trying to get past its brother, broken but still longer. The Blood Weeper's eyes welled red as he blocked the attacks.

Can't beat me without the anger, can you? Come on.

She feinted, trying to get his guard down. A line of fire ripped down her right side as she overextended and he slashed her thigh.

He took a step back and circled, holding the *katana* before him in a two-handed grip. She shifted her weight and hopped awkwardly. Blood dripped down her leg and spattered in the wet sand. He hobbled, but she could hardly stand. An idea formed.

"When you sleep, do you dream of a highway?"

He scowled.

"You're flying through the air, heading into the tall grass."

His head lowered.

"You're laying there, a sack of broken bones, and what's your final thought?"

Kikuchiyo shook his head from side to side.

"That you were just killed because instead of making out with you, your sweetie was giving some jerk a hand job."

The blood at the corners of his eyes filled and slid down his face.

Got you.

He leapt in with a shout. Jasmine threw the *wakizashi* in his face and grabbed at her belt. Kikuchiyo easily knocked the sword away and turned in time to deflect the glass vial Jasmine launched at his head. He batted the vial aside, and for a split second, Kikuchiyo's eyes lit with victory before turning to terror as the open vial's contents spread over his face.

Jasmine opened her hand and dropped the stopper.

Kikuchiyo retreated, wiping at his face. The *katana*'s broken tip shook as the tremors took him. Jasmine limped to Ryan and took a vial from her pouch, wetting her fingertip with the blood and pressing it to his forehead. Kikuchiyo cried out in Ryan's voice. He stumbled towards her, pawing at his morphing face and waving the *katana* before him.

Jasmine threw the *wakizashi* aside.

"Kikuchiyo, wait," she said.

The samurai's face rearranged itself into Ryan's confused features.

"Not my blood," she said and nodded at Ryan. "Before I came out, I filled the vial with some of his."

At her feet, Ryan gasped and his eyes blinked open. He stared into his own face then at the *katana*.

"Ryan, meet the Blood Weeper," she said.

Ryan sniffed. "Kill her."

Kikuchiyo looked between them, sword wavering.

"There's a blood link between you," she said to Ryan. "Right now, either one of you can be Ryan," she said.

"What?" Ryan cried. His face tightened in concentration. Kikuchiyo frowned and took a step forward, setting the *katana*'s broken tip to Ryan's throat.

"Stop that," Kikuchiyo said.

Ryan glanced to the *wakizashi,* just out of reach. Jasmine nudged it farther away with her foot.

"You can't control him any longer, Ryan."

He watched the sword. "Without me you're just unguided rage, Kikuchiyo."

"Every night, the same dream, the crash. You float away, I am left behind," Kikuchiyo said.

"Except when I stay and you get to float away, Kikuchiyo. That's always been our deal. Who's going to hold all the pain for you if I'm gone? Her?" Ryan scowled. "I'm the only one that can take it from you."

The samurai's face was like stone.

He blinked and a blood tear fell.

The *katana* twisted, breaking skin.

Ryan turned away from his avatar and glared at her instead.

"I hate you."

The *katana* withdrew. Kikuchiyo threw it to the sand.

He knelt and nodded at the blood vial. Jasmine held it out to him.

"Jas, don't!" Ryan shouted and reached for it.

Kikuchiyo shoved him away and poured the blood into a cupped hand, then dipped a finger in the pool and wiped the corners of his eyes. Seconds later, both men shouted with one voice and fell to the sand.

Jasmine went to the samurai and rolled him over. His face was his own once again.

"He is gone," Kikuchiyo said. "I am... empty."

He stared at the sand, saying nothing. Jasmine glanced at Ryan's body, unmoving but still breathing. She sat next to Kikuchiyo and waited, this man who had killed all her friends and tried killing her several times. She tried summoning up anger, but it wouldn't stick. She saw a hollow man, broken. After a few minutes, Kikuchiyo sat up, stared into the wind and wept blood-free tears.

"I am now without purpose," he said. "I should have died."

"Because Ryan left you?" Jasmine sniffed. She looked over to where her brother remained passed out on the sand.

"It is my duty to die." He lowered his head and whispered. "I cannot control the anger."

"Who told you that? Ryan? Wait here."

She returned to him with the *katana* and the *wakizashi*, placing them before him. When she faced him, his eyes darted to the swords, measuring the distance. For a moment, Jasmine thought he would just snatch one up and behead her before she could blink. Instead he brought his eyes forward and stared at the swirling water.

"You were never a samurai."

Kikuchiyo flinched as if she had slapped him, but he only gave a curt nod and grunted.

"That's not what I mean. This whole land is made up of the bullshit in Ryan's head and is about as stable, including this role he dreamed up for you. Your samurai ideal? It's a cartoon caricature of a B-grade movie cliche."

Kikuchiyo looked to the cloud-killer maelstrom.

"You already knew that, I think," she said.

"For me, there was only duty and its release from the dream. No other path."

"I'll give you a choice right now. This world is tearing itself apart. I can fix most of it myself, but not all of it. I could use your help."

"Betray one god for another?"

"No. This is your own path. Make the choice to help, or not. When I'm done there will be no more gods but I suspect there will still be evil men."

They watched The Maw's twin maelstroms swirl, Jasmine making sure she was still on dry land and not mindlessly heading into the water. He suddenly got up and brushed himself off, regaining a bit of his arrogance even though his wet clothes sagged and wrinkles plastered themselves to his body. Hair wisps tangled in the wind and he held out a hand.

"Come. Your brother will wake soon."

"Don't forget your swords."

He looked back at them, stuck into the sand. "I won't," he said, and turned his back on them.

She took his hand, rough with calluses, and followed, leaving the swords behind them.

30

Between them, Jasmine and Kikuchiyo got Ryan's unconscious form into the half-finished boat and pushed it along wooden rails to the water's edge. Ryan's color looked better and the open wounds sealed themselves as the bow hit the water. He let out a moan as something in his hip crunched.

"It grows larger," Kikuchiyo said, nodding at The Maw.

Jasmine nodded. "It calls to my brother and me."

"Will the dreams stop?" he asked.

"I don't know how much of him—of us—will be left behind. I hope not much if at all."

"All passages leave a mark."

Jasmine nodded. "Perhaps they do." She jerked her head back towards the desert. "Will you see to them?"

Kikuchiyo bent at the waist, giving her a military bow without taking his eyes from hers.

"I told you, you're not a samurai."

"Then whatever I am, I am."

She smiled. "Good luck, Kikuchiyo."

"And to you, Jasmine."

They pushed the boat into the water, and she scrambled in. The sea pulled and tossed her about as she crawled over to her brother, who looked relaxed. It reminded her of a day at their favorite theme park.

They rode the log flume all afternoon, sometimes waiting in line so long their soggy clothes had dried despite Florida's humid summers. The ride was so cheesy, with animatronic animals singing and acting out stories along the way like a reverse Mystery Play, but the cool water coupled with the speed and frequent splashes relieved the sweltering heat. The ride's best part came with the long climb at the end, building anticipation until you reached the top and got that terrifying glimpse before plummeting into the water for your final soaking.

The ride had a camera timed to go off just as the riders saw the pool below and the car had pulled enough momentum to give them a sinking feeling in their stomach. Most screamed, either in terror or joy. At the end of the ride, after you got out, little TV screens showed the riders their terror, their excitement, or whatever.

Then on the last ride, Ryan put his arms back behind his head and closed his eyes, looking like he was having the world's most pleasant dream just as the camera flashed. Jasmine didn't notice until the picture popped up on the screen.

"You dork," she laughed. There was her brother, a vision of serenity in the middle of chaos. The camera had caught her looking straight at the lens, with her mouth wide open in mid-scream.

"You should have flashed your boobs," he said. "We could have turned it into a postcard."

"You are such a perv," she said and elbowed him in the ribs. He had the decency to grunt as her elbow connected, but not enough to look sorry, or even rub at them later.

"We should get it anyway."

Ryan shook his head. "Nah. As long as you and I remember, it's enough. Besides, it's like ten dollars. I'd rather have an ice cream."

"I'm buying the picture," she said.

"Suit yourself, but I'm not sharing my ice cream."

She got the picture and after some cajoling, a bit of Ryan's cone too.

They hit the whitecaps, and Ryan moaned as water splashed his face. His eyes opened and glanced back at the beach where Kikuchiyo knelt *seiza,* watching them.

"I forgot how much it hurt—the accident, Kelly, all of it. No wonder I couldn't control him at the end, if I ever controlled him at all."

"How do you feel?" she asked.

"I ache, but it's a good ache, you know?"

"You sound different."

He tilted his head and gave the slightest shrug. "Maybe," he said. He stared at the swirling mist. "We'll just wake up at the tree house, Jas. I've died a few times here and it gets harder to fight your way free each time."

"At least we'll be together, right?"

A foot of water flooded the boat, gushing in over unfinished rails and seeping through unsealed cracks. Ryan tried getting up but collapsed. "Turn us back."

"No."

The current picked up, and the mist cooled their faces. The sawing wild pig sound grew louder and the boat began circling.

"We're caught now."

"It'll be okay," she said and grabbed his hand.

The boat completed a circuit, then another. Above them, the sky swirled in the opposite direction, pulling at the air around them. They spun faster, listing to the side and falling into the swirling bowl. They orbited a churning black hole at the maelstrom's center. The boat's hull creaked and popped.

"I hate dying," Ryan said. "It hurts so much."

"I know."

"When we wake up, I'm never going to let you forget this."

The holes in her mind filled in. The sarcasm in her stretched its arms and roared.

"Yeah, we'll paint 'Jasmine was wrong' in big letters on the tree house walls, along with 'Ryan can't keep it in his pants.' Whattya think?"

"I'm sorry."

"I know."

They tossed about as the boat broke up around them. Jasmine held onto her brother with both hands as they were thrown into the air. She closed her eyes and took a deep breath, waiting for the cold plunge.

It didn't come.

She opened her eyes as she floated and twisted in the wind with her brother. Ryan's eyes were wide and looking down at the wooden pieces disappearing into the maelstrom's frothy maw. They rose higher, above the water and gaining speed.

They looked up at the same time to the clear blue circle surrounded by swirling clouds. A pinprick of light formed, growing larger as they approached.

Ryan's hand crushed hers.

"Don't let go," Ryan said.

"I won't."

The sawing sound faded, replaced by whistling wind.

"I'm scared."

She met his eyes and the last hole in her head filled. Fear ran down her spine and settled deep in her bowels.

"Me too, Ryan. Me too."

The light, warm and enveloping, grew too bright for eyes. Ryan's crushing grip faded though neither of them had let go. Her ears tickled with the sound of a guitar playing something vaguely bluesy and entirely familiar. She wondered if Ryan heard it too.

EPILOGUE

Kikuchiyo the Ronin lowered his hand from his eyes. Clouds billowed over calm waters and drifted lazily to the horizon. He rose and brushed the sand from his knees, striding over to the swords stuck in the sand. The *daishō*, the long and the short, felt empty in his hands, mere pieces of metal and no longer the living extensions of his soul. He turned them over, mindful of the razor-sharp edges they still held. He considered leaving them in the sand but walked from the beach with the *daishō* tucked into his sash.

The gods healed the land in their leaving, but the world remained littered with their mistakes, avatars and wicked men who desired many things but craved power. He had been challenged with a new path to walk, and he had accepted. He did not know the path's shape, only that he would follow it to the end.

BONUS FEATURES

But wait, there's more!

If you made it this far, I'm guessing you enjoyed this trip into the Badlands (that, or you're a completist, which I totally respect). To continue exploring the mysterious Badlands, get the next book right now.

Get Enter the Samurai

Get The Good Stuff!

Would you like to know more about deaders and necros? If you sign up for the mailing list I'll send you a free ebook you can't get anywhere else: Black Betty: A Badlands Story, featuring your favorite necrosonic engineer, Helgo.

Building a relationship with my readers and talking about stories are two of my favorite things about writing. I occasionally send out updates on new releases, special offers, and other tasty bits relating to the series I'm writing.

Sign up at WadePeterson.com

If you just want to do the simplest thing

If all that is too much but you enjoyed my book, please consider leaving a review. Reviews are the lifeblood of indie books like this and I would consider it a personal favor — just a quick star rating with a sentence or two can make a huge difference in convincing others to give this book a try.

I am on a quest to get 100 reviews of this book and I can only do it with your help.

Of course I'll leave a review!

AUTHOR'S NOTES

Badlands Born and Badlands Cursed was originally conceived as a single NaNoWriMo novel but the fever-dream refused to be constrained by a mere 50,000 words and 30 days of attention. In the years that followed I rearranged and split the story into into two books, the first telling the story of Jasmine coming into her powers and the second about how she struggled to remain human. It's my own love letter and critique of the 1980s I grew up in, the awesome absurdity of what popular culture was etching into my teenage brain and the deprogramming I've gone through in the years since.

I was worried the story would end with Jasmine and Ryan, but the weird magic of the Badlands didn't disappear with the twins and other characters emerged with their hands raised wanting their stories to be told too. If you'd like to know more about how Helgo met Black Betty, or why Captain Beaumont trusted Chevket, I've got you.

Tag me on social media or send me an email letting me know what interests you — I'm excited to write more Badlands stories and you can help shape the next one.

Wade Peterson

May 2020

<<<<>>>>

ABOUT THE AUTHOR

Wade Peterson is a man. He's pretty sure he is, anyway. When he's not writing, he's busy unlocking the secrets of Texas barbecue, wrangling two demonic cats, tormenting his kids with dad jokes, and agreeing wholeheartedly with his wife's wine selection for the evening.

Click on the icons below to follow Wade on social media for updates, fun pictures, and the occasional cat video. Of course the best stuff is at wadepeterson.com (just saying).